Trailer
GET YOUR KICKS!

BOOK THREE OF THE TIME TRAVEL TRAILER

by
Karen Musser Nortman

Cover Design by Hell Yes Design Studio

Dedicated to anyone who relives special moments in their dreams

If you ever plan to motor west,
Travel my way, take the highway that is best.
Get your kicks on route sixty-six.

Bobby Troup

I'll be seeing you
In all the old familiar places
That this heart of mine embraces

Irving Khal

TABLE OF CONTENTS

CHAPTER ONE
Lynne

I DUMPED TWO SACKS of groceries on the kitchen counter and scrambled through my purse for my buzzing phone.

"Hello?"

"Ms. McBriar? Herb Branson here."

I searched my memory. "Yes?" A client? No one that I was currently working with. "Um, what can I do for you?"

He launched into an explanation.

"I run the RiteWay RV Sales and Museum over in Illinois. You brought your vintage camper here for display last fall?"

"Oh, yes! Sorry—it threw me for a minute. Is there a problem?" I felt a nudge of dread. I hoped he wasn't calling with an offer to buy the trailer, because I wasn't about to part with it. And not just for sentimental reasons.

1

He laughed. "No—no problem. It's been a very popular exhibit. Lots of older people have commented that it takes them back in time."

You have no idea.

"No," he continued, "I'm calling because a friend of mine who runs a dealership in Amarillo, Texas has asked to borrow it. He also has a museum—larger than mine, and is holding a vintage camper rally this summer. He has been looking for a Covered Wagon for years, but has never been able to find one."

"Texas!" I realized as I said it that I sounded like I had never been out of Iowa.

"You wouldn't have to do anything. We would haul it down there and bring it back at the end of the rally."

"Oh, I think. . ." I knew what I thought but didn't want to share it with good old Herb.

"Say, I've got a customer here I need to talk to. Think about it, why don't you, and call me back tomorrow sometime?"

I took a breath. "Okay, that would be fine. I have your number."

"Great! That will give you a chance to think of any other questions. Talk to you tomorrow."

After I hung up, I leaned against the counter. This would not work. If someone else towed that trailer to Texas, what if they decided to sleep in it? They would likely wake up in 1937 or some other time period.

My beautiful vintage camper—that I had purchased

from my friend Ben Walker and carefully restored, that I and my daughter Dinah had taken several memorable trips in — that camper time-traveled.

After a particularly scary trip the previous summer, I decided that time travel carried too many risks, and that the camper needed to be put out of commission. Destroying it was not the answer. My family and Ben and Minnie Walker and I hit on the scheme of loaning it to a museum. We reasoned that if I didn't sell it and it was locked in a display somewhere, no one else would encounter its special talents.

I felt dampness at the back of my waist and stood, remembering that I hadn't yet put the ice cream away — or any of the other groceries. And I needed to get some supper started for Kurt and Dinah. She had a softball game scheduled right after supper.

I spent the next hour throwing together a pasta salad and warming some rolls from the local bakery. All the while I mulled over Herb Branson's request. By far the simplest solution was to say no, but I needed to come up with a reasonable excuse.

Kurt got home first and gingerly hugged me while looking askance at the paring knife in my hand. We were just getting used to living in the same house again after separation for a couple of years, counseling, and more than one setback. As a result of the counseling, Kurt had quit the job he hated and started his own software business.

"You aren't planning on using that on me are you?"

"Not today. Not so far anyway. How was your day?" I washed my hands.

"Great! I have a new client—a young man I met at that conference last month. And yours?"

"Fine." I turned around to face him. "I just got off the phone, though, with Herb Branson."

"Who's Herb Branson? A boyfriend I don't know about? I—" He was cut off as the door slammed and footsteps stomped up the half flight of steps to the kitchen.

Sixteen-year-old Dinah dropped her backpack on the counter and whipped her mop of hair back from her face. Her face was flushed and her mouth set in a grim line.

"What's wrong?"

"Tish!"

"Tish what?" Kurt asked. Tish had been her best friend since grade school.

She put her fists on her hips and looked at us like we were some kind of stupid. "She quit softball." Dinah switched to a sing-songy voice meant to imitate her friend. "She's afraid she'll hurt her hands and won't be able to play the piano."

"That's called setting priorities." Kurt shrugged. "But why didn't she think of that before the season started?"

"Exactly! That's what *I* asked her! Now I won't have *anyone* to talk to at practice or on road trips."

I knew Kurt and I were thinking that perhaps at

practice she could concentrate on practice, but that suggestion wouldn't be well-received.

We raised our eyebrows at each other as she stomped out of the kitchen and headed up to her room. This too would pass. A couple of years earlier, Dinah's belligerent and sassy behavior nearly was the end of me, but we were seeing fewer and fewer of these episodes. Knock on wood.

"Supper's in about five minutes!" I called after her.

A grudging reply. "Yeah."

As I passed the bowl of pasta to Kurt, he said, "Who's this guy that called?"

I wasn't sure if I wanted to include Dinah in this discussion "Herb Branson."

She perked up immediately. "From the RV place? What did he want? Did something happen to the camper?"

Now why could *she* remember that guy's name when neither of us could?

"Yes. Nothing's happened to it. But some friend of his wants to borrow it for his display in Texas this summer. He's a dealer too and has a museum."

Kurt put down his fork. "How would they get it there?"

"That's my concern. He said they would 'haul it down there' but I didn't ask if he meant on a flat bed or something. If they plan to tow it, I wouldn't want them to sleep in it."

"They would get a surprise for sure," Dinah agreed.

Kurt looked thoughtful. "Maybe we should offer to take it. Make a little family vacation out of it."

I was astonished. Kurt had *no* positive feelings about that camper and had been only too glad to get rid of it.

He continued. "My new client is a biker—rides with a group of video-gamers on weekends, and last year they took a trip on Route 66. It sounded like a fun idea."

Dinah grinned. "On motorcycles? Cool."

He shook his head. "I mean, making the same trip by car. Where in Texas does he want to take the trailer?"

"Amarillo, I think he said."

"That's right on 66."

"Are you serious?" I still couldn't believe what he was saying.

"You mean about taking it down there? Sure. That way you wouldn't have to worry about what someone else is doing with it. We would sleep in motels, of course, not in the camper,"

"We could add some new stuff back in and then sleep in it," Dinah said.

We were by no means sure how the trailer time traveled, but my main theory was that it was connected to the age of the most recent remodel.

"I think I like the motel idea better," I said. "Let's not tempt fate any more with that thing."

Kurt nodded. "I agree. When does it need to be down there?"

"I didn't think to ask—I was so taken back by the request and panicked at the thought of someone else traveling in it. I'm supposed to call him back tomorrow so I'll get the particulars—and how long he needs it to be there. Because there's also the issue of getting it back."

Kurt thought a moment. "Hmmm. I could go back to get it." He grinned. "I am my own boss, you know."

CHAPTER TWO

Lynne

THE NEXT DAY, I called Herb Branson during a break between two clients. I told him about our decision to take the camper to Texas as part of a family trip.

"When does it need to be there and for how long?" I asked.

"The rally is in late June. Starts the 22nd I believe, and I'm sure he would want it a couple of days before that. Then I think he would like to display it through July. Would that work? Really, it's no problem for me to get it down there."

"My husband is anxious to drive Route 66 and sees this as the perfect opportunity. We'll decide when we need to start, and I'll get back to you, okay?"

"Great! I'll let my friend know and email you the particulars. Have a nice day." Herb hung up.

I hung up and hoped this would work.

THAT NIGHT AFTER SUPPER, we got out the atlas and fired up the laptop to plan our trip. Kurt found several websites highlighting stops along the famous old highway with photos of surviving buildings that housed gas stations, diners, and motels in the heyday of the Mother Road.

Even Dinah was fascinated. "Wow! That's a *gas station*? It looks like only one car could get gas at a time."

"Right," Kurt said, "but not as many cars on the road in those days."

"Look at these old photos. People dressed up a lot more for trips back then." I pointed out women in dresses and heels, sometimes even with hats and gloves. Men wore dress shirts and ties and hats.

Kurt was making a list of the stops we might want to make, so that we could gauge how long we wanted to spend on the trip. He leaned over to look at the photos. "Those are great. Wouldn't it be fun to see what it was really like?" Then he shut up as he realized what he said and looked at me.

"No," I said.

"I wasn't suggesting anything—it's just that after I said it, it dawned on me that we actually could—"

"No," I repeated. "There're too many problems—"

He held up his hands. "I know, I know."

Dinah looked from one to the other. "What? You mean we could go back, say to 1937 and drive Route 66 when it was almost new? That would be awesome."

9

"No." I sighed, tired of repeating myself.

"But—," Dinah began

I cut her off. "You weren't with me last year on that trip to Paulie's Shoots. Too many things changed—things I never would have thought that could be affected by my trying to save Beverly's life."

Kurt leaned back in his chair, stretched out his legs, and stuck his hands in his pockets. His hair fell a little over his forehead. For a moment he looked like a typical high school boy slouching in English class.

"I'm not saying we should, but just playing the devil's advocate, we wouldn't be changing anything—just observing."

I stared at him. "I can't believe you are even considering a plan like that."

Dinah, too, was rather shocked. She and I were the ones who had experimented the most with the camper. Kurt at first disbelieved us and then argued adamantly against any further use of it. Last summer he wanted to destroy it. I would have gone along with that except for one question. Ben Walker, the friend I had bought it from, had used it to save his wife Minnie's life. If we destroyed the trailer, none of us knew what that would do to the time line changes that had been instigated with it. You just can't Google that.

"I know. I can't either. But my little taste of time travel when we went to get Dinah was intriguing—just to see people and places in our recent history come to life."

Two years ago, in the most rebellious year of her teens so far, Dinah had used the trailer to travel back to 1937 and met her own great-grandmother. She intended to throw a scare into us, and she succeeded. Kurt and I followed because we feared she might not be able to get back to us.

He continued. "It seems like this might be the perfect opportunity to use it without repercussions. If we could go back in time—maybe just before we cross Missouri, and then return to the present as we go into Oklahoma, we could get a little flavor of that time."

I ran both hands through my hair, pulling it back from my face. "You aren't considering all of the problems here. We couldn't travel farther than one tank of gas, right? Because the Jeep wouldn't run on 1937 gas. They didn't even *have* Jeeps then so that would raise a lot of eyebrows and questions. And what if we couldn't get back?"

Kurt shook his head. "You're right, I suppose."

WE DISCUSSED OUR ROUTE for several nights. Time traveling wasn't mentioned again, but I knew Kurt and Dinah were itching to consider it further. Finally one night Kurt looked up from a map.

"We could plan our time trip to be within a one tank range of the Jeep and take along a gas can for emergencies."

"What time trip? We agreed that it isn't a good idea."

11

"C'mon, Mom," Dinah said. "Just driving down the road, we don't have to interact with anyone else—we wouldn't change anything. It would be very educational for me." She grinned as if she thought she had already won.

"There are *lots* of educational things we could do that wouldn't be nearly as risky. Besides, it isn't fair for you two to gang up on me."

"Majority rule." Dinah peered up at me from under a veil of hair.

"But," I pointed at her, "it's *my* camper."

Kurt grimaced but didn't say anything. He knew I had more experience with time travel in the classic trailer, not all of it good. Some of it downright scary, in fact.

But Dinah wasn't giving up. "Can I buy it? I saved quite a bit of money working at the pool last summer. I'll give you what you paid for it."

Kurt laughed, and I couldn't hold it back either. "You imp! That's not the issue and you know it."

She shrugged and got up from the table. "Well, this obviously isn't a democracy, so I'm going to go do my homework."

I went back to my computer where I had pulled up information on Route 66, but I felt Kurt's eyes on me. I looked up. "What?"

"Nothing. I'm just trying some mind control."

"Oh, for heaven's sake!" I closed the laptop. "You and Dinah are incorrigible. I thought after the last discussion, you told me you agreed with my concerns."

"I know."

"But you want to do it anyway."

"I just think we can do it without getting in trouble or causing any changes. Sleep in it, travel for one day, and sleep in it again to get back to the present."

"Kurt. . ." My gut told me there was a flaw in this argument, but my brain wasn't coming up with anything. "I don't know. Let me think about it some more."

"That's all I ask." He leaned over and squeezed my shoulder.

I smiled, but couldn't quite wrap my head around Kurt's change of direction on that trailer. I knew he had become fascinated with the old Route 66 highway and the historical developments around it. He had picked up books at the library and the bookstore and spent quite a bit of time at home researching on his laptop.

As if reading my mind, he said, "I might as well confess. I'm thinking about developing a video game based on the old Route 66. That's what my new client and I are working on. There's a couple of others out there, but I've got some ideas on a different twist."

"Ah. And if you could experience it in its prime, you would have a leg up."

He nodded. "What do you think?"

"You know what I think. But that puts a slightly different light on it." I held up a hand. "It doesn't erase my concerns, but I will think about it. Maybe we should talk to Ben."

"I'm willing to do that. And then make a decision."

"You would go along with what he recommends?"

He sighed. "Yes."

I WAS RELIEVED. I felt fairly certain that Ben and his wife Minnie would discourage this scheme. They had been all in favor of placing it in the museum where no one would experience its time travel abilities by accident.

We called the Walkers, and all three of us drove out to see them the next Saturday morning. Ben and Minnie were one of those cute couples who should be in a Hallmark holiday movie. A basket of kittens waylaid Dinah near the back steps. I ignored her plaintive "We should get a cat!" and followed Kurt inside. Minnie had wonderful coffee and cranberry-orange scones ready for us.

We chatted for a few minutes about upcoming church events and rehashed the local gossip. I finished my scone and pushed my plate away. "Those are delicious, Minnie. I'm surprised Ben hasn't put on a hundred pounds since you got married."

Ben patted his little round tummy. "I would, but she watches what I eat—like a hawk. I have a feeling you have a special purpose in your visit today. Something with the camper?"

I nodded. "Isn't it always?" I told him about the call from Herb Branson and his request.

Kurt then took over and explained his interest in Route 66.

Ben and Minnie both listened closely, nodding once in awhile. I had talked to them before I made a trip to Missouri the previous year, and Ben had cautioned me very strongly. He was worried about my safety and pointed out that the effects of even small changes on the timeline are largely unknown and could endanger our loved ones as well as people we've never met. I was sure he would remind us both of the same possibilities.

"Well, that's quite a project, Kurt. I've never played video games, but you will have to teach me when you get that one done. As they said in our day 'sounds cool, man.' I don't see a big problem with this trip. If like you say, you keep your time trip to one day and only observe, I would think you'd be fine."

"But, you always—" I started, unable to formulate my thoughts coherently.

"Lynne," Kurt cautioned.

I remembered his promise and felt obligated to keep my side of it as well. I stayed silent.

Ben tilted his head toward me. "I take it you don't agree with me."

I shrugged. "There're a lot of concerns for me. The Jeep—we won't be able to gas it up and of course there weren't any Jeeps until after the War. If we would break down or something—" I shrugged again.

"Does your Jeep break down often?" Minnie asked.

15

"Never has," I admitted.

"You have to do what you feel comfortable with," Ben said. "I just meant if you drive and don't interact with anyone, you should be okay. It would be fun..." he added wistfully.

Kurt got up. "Thanks very much for the input...and the scones. We'd better get Dinah away from those cats before she insists on adopting one or two."

I stood to follow. "Better check her pockets." Inside, I was in turmoil.

"HERE'S THE THING," Kurt said as we drove home. "We could pick up some time-appropriate stuff—say, mid 50s, because of the Jeep. If we get down there and you are still very uncomfortable with the time travel, we don't have to go through with it."

I gave up. I really didn't have a good argument against the plan and felt a little better with Ben's reassurance. Kurt's business had been his dream, and as we tried to rebuild our marriage, I needed to support that. "All right, I'll go along with that."

"And when we get back," Dinah said from the back seat, "we could get one of those kittens. I bet Ben and Minnie would give us one."

I dropped my head back against the head rest. "Please. One life-changing decision at a time."

CHAPTER THREE

Lynne

ONE ORDER OF BUSINESS was license plates. I had picked up several sets of plates from the 50s at a local junk shop when Dinah and I were first trying out the trailer. I put the plates in an empty tote. Meanwhile, Kurt buried himself in the atlas, guide books, and laptop—searching for a place to begin and end the time travel segment.

I was working in the kitchen the next Saturday morning when I heard a "Yoohoo!" from the driveway.

Kurt went to the side door. "Linda! C'mon in—the coffee's still hot." He led my mother up into the kitchen.

She gave me a hug, and asked about Dinah. "I haven't seen any of you in a couple of weeks and thought I'd better stop and see what was going on."

"Dinah's not up yet—it's only 10:00 and that's a little

early for her." I caught a guilty look on Kurt's face. Apparently he thinks Mother can read minds. "Here's some coffee—take it to the dining room table and I'll be right there."

As she left the room, Kurt whispered "Are you going to tell her about the trip?"

"The trip, of course. Not the other." I dried my hands and carried my coffee and the cookie jar into the dining room.

Mother stood at the other side of the table, peering down at the license plates in the plastic tote.

"What's all this?" she said. "Didn't you get these for that old camper? I thought you got rid of it."

I looked at Kurt. Mother knew about the time travel because we asked for her help when Dinah disappeared into the past.

We had to tell her what we were thinking. "Have a seat and we'll explain," I said. We told her about the call from Herb Branson and our decision to deliver the trailer ourselves to avoid any 'mishaps.'

"Sounds like a good idea. And it should be safe enough just pulling down the road. So what are the license plates for?"

Mom didn't fall of the turnip truck yesterday.

"Kurt?" I wasn't going to take the heat for this. Mother feared the worst when we went back to the Thirties to bring our daughter back. No way she would go along with time travel just for research for a video game.

Kurt told her about his interest in Route 66 and the desire to experience a bit of the famous highway in its prime.

Mother's eyes lit up. "We used to drive down 66 to visit my dad's family in Arkansas—it was so exciting, all of the diners and motels. Seemed like everyone in America was on that road. Oh, I would love to go too!"

Am I the only sane one in my family?

WE TRIED TO DISCOURAGE HER, and she put on her martyred look. The I-suppose-I-would-just-be-a-burden routine. The only guilt worse than what your kids lay on you is what your parents drop on your head.

I mentioned that the Jeep wasn't the most comfortable of rides, and she talked about how Dinah would be going away to college in another year, and it would be her last chance to spend much time with her, uncomfortable or not.

Really, Mother? She isn't going to school on Mars.

Kurt said he didn't know how long we would be gone, and she just said, "I'm retired, remember?"

There wasn't much I could say to that.

And finally, I thought, if we disappeared into the deep dark past, we would all be together—Mom wouldn't be left back here alone. I had effectively been steamrollered.

THE BIGGEST ISSUE was how to get back to 1951 or '52. Mom was born in 1953 and it would simplify things if we went back before that. We didn't know for sure, but Minnie thought that if you were alive in a time frame, you revert to your age at the time. We didn't relish the idea of dealing with a newborn even for a day without supplies, etc. There was something just too weird about me taking care of my mother as an infant.

The camper was a 1937 Covered Wagon. The exterior was dark brown leatherette with a white canvas roof that had been sealed from the weather. Inside, the walls were covered with wood and the cabinets all had refrigerator-style latches.

Besides the couch and dinette booth which both could be made into beds, the little trailer featured a half-bath, unusual for its day. When I first bought the trailer from Ben, I began to restore it by removing layers of flooring and wall coverings. Each time we took it out and slept in it, we would wake up the year of the previous remodel. Last summer I had been able to take it back ten years by installing some carpet that had been manufactured in that year. If we were going to control the year of the time change, we needed something from 1952 that we could affix in the trailer.

We discussed our options. It wasn't too hard finding ten-year-old carpet but locating flooring that we knew for sure had been manufactured in 1952 seemed like a stretch. Mom came for supper, and we discussed the problem.

"What do you think you need?" Mom asked.

"We don't know anything for sure, but it seems to take something that is attached to the camper that was manufactured in the year you want to return to. Last summer I found used carpet that actually had the manufacturing date stamped on the back. But, I only needed to go back ten years. We need something more than sixty years old for this trip."

Mother laid down her fork and rested her chin on her hands. "Hmmm. 1952. I'm pretty sure that's when my parents redid the bathroom in this house. Mother always said she told Daddy she would not have any babies until she had a modern bathroom, and I was born the next year."

Our little frame house had been in my family since my great grandparents were married. My parents lived here until Kurt and I bought it in 2000.

"We could hardly put the bathtub or stool in that camper," Kurt said.

"No," Mom said, "but what about the medicine cabinet? Did you ever replace it?"

"We were going to but never got it done." Kurt looked a little guilty when he glanced at me. No reason to — we've both always had more big ideas about remodeling the house than ambition to carry it out.

"Maybe now's the time," I said. "Maybe it was fate that we still have it."

Dinah twirled spaghetti on her fork. "I thought you didn't believe in fate."

21

"I believe in whatever is convenient. At Christmas, I always believe in Santa. Just in case."

"Don't forget the jewelry," Dinah said.

My mother looked at her, confused. "Jewelry?"

"Each time we went back, one of us was wearing jewelry from that year. The first pieces came from a box Dinah found in the camper. Then when we wanted to come back, we didn't wear it. So we need to find something from '52."

"I'll look in the box, but how do we know the exact age?" Dinah said.

"That's the problem. After supper, bring it down and we'll look."

Kurt fixated on the cabinet. "It would be best if we could measure the camper to see if that cabinet will fit. Otherwise, we'll have to come up with something else."

"How about a little road trip to talk to Herb Branson this Saturday? I can use the excuse that I need to arrange picking it up, get directions, and so on, and you can sneak in and measure?" I said.

"That should work," he said

As Mother and Dinah carried dishes out so I could rinse and load them in the dishwasher, Mother asked, "So how do you decide where you will try and make the time change?"

"I'm thinking we should try this one day time switch in Missouri. We need to find campgrounds or deserted locations that are available both now and back in 1952."

"Isn't that kind of hard?"

I dried my hands. "It can be. I usually look for a park that has been around at least that long, but sometimes even that is hard to find out."

Mother nodded but didn't say anything else.

Kurt turned from stashing leftovers in the refrigerator. "There's a campground just past St. Louis that advertises itself as the oldest campground on Route 66. If we filled the gas tank there, we could easily make Springfield the next day."

Dinah went upstairs for the shoebox of costume jewelry that she had found in one of the storage compartments right after I bought the trailer from Ben. She poured the contents out on the table.

"Is this everything?" I asked.

"Yeah. I've been afraid to wear any of it even if I'm not in the camper." She smiled sheepishly.

Mother and I pawed through the pile. "I don't know how we can tell the year of any of this," I said.

Dinah opened the laptop, did a search for 1952 jewelry, and pored over the screen. "There were lots of bracelets and necklaces made out of real coins. Did you see any of that in there?"

"No, but that would be a way to be sure of the date," Mother paused and looked at us. "I remember my mom having a bracelet with coins. I was fascinated with it when I was little. I'll look in the attic when I get home. I can't imagine that I would have thrown that out."

"We need to go back to Violet's for some clothes, too," Dinah said. "You got rid of everything we bought two years ago. None of it would fit me any more, anyway."

Second Hand Violet's was a local vintage clothing store. Mom clapped her hands at the suggestion. "Goody! I love that place."

I laughed. "Are you sure most of that stuff isn't yours?"

She gave me a light slap on the arm. "Lynne! That's very disrespectful. As you know, I'm not that old!"

Dinah had gone back to the laptop to search for 1952 fashions. "Oooh, Daddy needs a hat!"

Mother looked over her shoulder. "And some of those pleated trousers."

"Wait a minute," I said. "I thought we decided to only go back for one day and not interact with anyone. We don't need complete wardrobes."

Kurt joined us in the dining room. "We'll have to make bathroom stops and probably have lunch. So we each need at least one outfit. But you're right—we won't need much."

I got a little picture in the back of my mind of a camel's nose poking through the tent flap and Kurt, Dinah, and my mother pushing on his behind.

THE FOLLOWING SATURDAY we drove to Herb Branson's dealership in central Illinois. He gave me a printout from his friend's website of directions to the dealership in Amarillo and a phone number. He was anxious to get out of the office and home for some sort of family celebration.

"Would you mind if we go in the camper for a few minutes?" I asked.

He took his jacket off a wall hook and turned around. "Of course not. It's yours."

"Okay, we'll be back then in two weeks to pick it up." We all shook hands and he thanked us again for doing the transport.

We traipsed to the museum building and found our camper in the display. Herb and his employees had surrounded it with artificial turf and a small picket fence. A couple of vintage metal lawn chairs and an old metal cooler completed the scene.

Kurt led the way up the steps and once inside removed a rope that kept visitors in the entry area. Gripping the tape measure and a scrap of paper, with a pencil in his teeth, he stepped into the tiny bathroom. Mother, Dinah, and I followed. As he measured the space, he glanced over his shoulder at the three of us crowded around the bathroom door.

"Good thing I'm not doing heart surgery."

"We're just here to help you, Daddy," Dinah said.

"Right. Well, I think we can fit it in here. This mirror is in pretty bad shape anyway." He wrote on his little piece of paper, stuck the pencil behind his ear, and turned to face us. "Back! Back! Back!" He made a shooing motion to get us out of his way. "Monday, I'll go pick up a new cabinet for the bathroom at home, and we'll get the old one installed in here."

"I think I'll help pick out the new one," I said. Kurt is not known for his taste in interior design.

"Whatever."

CHAPTER FOUR

Lynne

BY OUR DEPARTURE DATE, I had tied up loose ends with my current clients and posted a notice on my website that my travel agency would be closed for three weeks. Kurt arranged for an internet connection, so he could keep working while we were gone. Since we did not plan to camp other than two nights, there wasn't much needed in the way of food.

Kurt did find a hat and a pair of pleated trousers at Violet's. Mother bought a housedress while Dinah and I opted for our own jeans with the cuffs rolled up and plaid blouses. Mother said our jeans weren't baggy enough, but I was okay with people thinking we were floozies for one day. Under pressure from Kurt, Dinah and I went back and bought sundresses with little short jackets. He was concerned that we might want to eat supper in a restaurant that didn't allow jeans. I thought we could just take sandwich materials in the camper.

Mother found a bracelet with several coins from the 50s dangling from it. We decided it was best to carefully remove the three that were dated after 1952.

Kurt continued to pore over maps and Internet stories about Route 66 and obsessed over the story of Times Beach, Missouri.

"It was intended as a resort town along the Merramac River. In the 20s, a St. Louis newspaper sold lots for $67.50 and you also got a six month subscription to the paper. But the Depression and gas rationing during World War II kind of killed the resort town idea. It became just a small blue collar town."

I sensed there was more to it to garner his attention. "And?"

He struck a thoughtful pose. "So glad you asked. The town was too poor to pave their dirt streets, and in the 70s they hired a contractor to spread oil to keep the dust down. The oil also included some industrial waste from nearby chemical plants that manufactured the components used in Agent Orange."

"What's Agent Orange?" Dinah asked.

"An herbicide used in the Vietnam War that has had lots of long term health affects on soldiers and civilians," I said.

"The problem for Times Beach was that the industrial waste was high in dioxin, which is very dangerous. Long story short, the town was evacuated, owners were bought out, the ground was remediated, and now it's a state park."

"I hope somebody got in trouble for all that," Dinah said.

Kurt shook his head. "None of it was illegal at the time."

"That stinks. None of it?"

"Nope. There weren't any laws or regulations against the dumping, and the guy that hauled it and sprayed the roads didn't know what was in it. The average person never heard of dioxin."

"Sooo," I said, "tell me what this means for our trip."

"I've studied maps of the park and maps of the town and found a spot where I think we can make the time change. We'll have to camp in the parking lot because this park doesn't have camping. We can see Times Beach as it was long before the contamination."

"There's a problem with that plan. I'm sure the park staff will check all the parking lots for stragglers before they close for the night."

"Hmmm. Didn't think of that. I'll look again at the Google Earth shots and see if there's a place we can pull off and kind of hide in the trees."

This plan gave me pause and did not assuage my reservations about the whole scheme. While Kurt searched the maps, I tried to identify what was bothering me the most. Even though I didn't begin to understand how the time travel thing worked, I had made several trips and returned successfully every time. Three trips the first summer had been in campgrounds that had been around long enough to serve both time periods. The fourth one had been from our back yard to a barn that had stood in the same spot eighty years earlier. The next summer—last year—I had made one trip, again in an old campground, spent a few days at another campground, and returned. Then I got it—what had been bothering me.

"Kurt," I said, interrupting his study, "there's something else. We're talking about moving the camper and coming back to the present in a different spot."

"What do you mean?"

"I haven't ever done that. I don't know if it would work. We know that some form of the camper stays in the present—like when Dinah traveled in it to 1937 but we still had it—or some version of it—in our back yard. I think we would probably have to go back to the same spot to come back to the present."

Kurt stared at me. I could tell he was trying to process this. One of the problems with time travel is that you end up thinking in circles and often don't get anywhere.

"Oh." He went back to his maps. After making some notes and checking distances on the laptop, he looked up. I hoped he was going to cancel this part of the plan, but no such luck.

"How about this? We still park there, the next

morning drive as far as Cuba to the Wagon Wheel restaurant for lunch and drive back. It will just add a day to our trip." He noticed the expression on my face. "What?"

I sat down at the table beside him. "I'm really nervous about this."

"Ben thought it would be fine."

"I know—I'm a little gun shy after my previous experiences. No one really knows—not even Ben— how it works, or all of the things that can go wrong. At least no one we know. Okay, let's do that half-day trip and get back to the park—or town—or whatever's there—as quick as we can."

ORIGINALLY WE WERE GOING to pick up the camper and head south but, considering that we needed to install the medicine cabinet, we decided to pick it up a day early, and bring it home to do the work. Of course, the installation was not without its frustrations, but finally Kurt was satisfied.

"At least all of the gouges are behind the cabinet, and when we put the mirror back up, it will cover any boo-boos. Don't forget to bring the old mirror along so we can change it back out."

I looked at him. "Yes, *one* of us should remember that." After all, this wasn't my idea.

WE MANAGED TO GET southwest of St. Louis with no

mishaps. Lunch at a truck stop drew lots of stares, admiring comments, and questions about the camper, but I had gotten used to that. Kurt and I took turns driving and declined Dinah's offer to spell us—she had gotten her license exactly two weeks before.

We reached the Route 66 State Park and parked near the Visitor's Center. The frame building was less imposing than many such structures—gray with white trim on its rows of mullioned windows—but Kurt informed me that it was formerly an inn called Steiny's

Kurt was like the proverbial kid at Christmas. We trailed him from exhibit to exhibit, perusing road signs, souvenirs, and photos.

Dinah leaned over a glass case and her surprise was evident. "This really is cool stuff."

"Duh," Kurt said.

She looked up and beamed. "Nobody likes a smart ass, Daddy."

"Watch your mouth, young lady." He grinned back at her.

We spent another hour looking around until Dinah announced she was "starving."

A SHORT DISTANCE AWAY we found a diner, obviously new, but decorated in the Fifties style.

Kurt locked up the Jeep. "This will get us in the mood."

It felt to me like sort of a Disney version of the Fifties,

but the burgers and fries served in baskets wrapped in cheery red checked paper were excellent. Dinah examined the choices on the jukebox and returned to our table.

"Wow—there were some really stupid song names back then. One called 'Sh-Boom'?"

"And like now all of the popular songs are deep and profound?" I asked.

"Whatever." Fortunately, the food arrived.

After we finished, we gassed up the Jeep and then headed back to the park. There were still a few hours of daylight left, so we left the trailer in the parking lot to hike a couple of the trails.

Kurt had picked up a park map at the visitor's center. "Let's head down this trail because it follows the river in a short distance."

As we walked along the river, Kurt explained that the trail would eventually wind up by one of the spots where the buildings from Times Beach had been buried. It was a perfect summer day and I managed to forget the possible issues we could face that night and enjoy the walk. The water was placid and waning light cast rippling shadows on the water. Wildflowers lined the bank, and the bluffs across the river provided backdrop.

"It doesn't look like an environmental disaster," I said.

"Not after twenty years and millions of dollars to clean it up," Kurt said. "Hundreds of millions."

Mother shook her head with unease. "It's just scary how many bad effects there have been with what seemed like good ideas at the time."

The path turned away from the river through some woods until it reached a huge open field.

"This is where they buried all of the homes and other buildings."

"What about the soil?" Dinah asked. "Is it still contaminated?"

Kurt shook his head. "They used a huge incinerator for about two years to sterilize it. C'mon, let's head back to the camper. It'll be dark soon, and we have to get the camper hidden before they close the gates and check the parking lots."

Shrubs lined the lot where we had parked. Behind them stood rows of trees planted in the last twenty years. We found an open spot through which Kurt was sure he could pull the camper and park it between the first two rows of pines. I wasn't sure of anything.

Dinah stood watch at the entrance to the parking lot while I directed Kurt into the hiding place. The shrubs along the lot masked the Jeep and trailer pretty well, especially since it was almost dark. We took advantage of restrooms on the opposite side of the lot.

To avoid making noise or having any lights on, we decided to sleep in our clothes and went to bed as soon as we were inside the camper. Kurt and I would sleep on the opened couch and Mother and Dinah in the converted dinette/bed.

"What if they do find us?" Dinah whispered. "What are we going to say?"

"Just that we couldn't afford a campground and thought we weren't bothering anyone," Kurt said.

Dinah frowned. "I don't know if they'll believe that."

"More than if we said we were trying to time travel," I told her.

"I guess you're right." She lay down and pulled a blanket over her.

I fastened the coin bracelet on my wrist and climbed in beside Kurt. Unfortunately every time I shifted in the slightest, trying to get comfortable, the bracelet clanked.

"Sounds like we have a ghost walking," my mother said in the dark, and Dinah started to giggle.

"Shhh," I said, holding the bracelet still with my other hand.

My caution only made Dinah's laughter worse, and Mother joined her. But they made a supreme effort and soon quieted.

I lay there for a long time, staring into the dark. About half an hour later, the windows brightened on the parking lot side with the dispersed glow of headlights. I held my breath but they were soon gone. The last time I looked at my watch, it was after 11:00.

CHAPTER FIVE

Lynne

I WOKE UP when Kurt sat up, pushed back one of the curtains, and peered out the window.

"I'll be damned," he said.

I rubbed my eyes and the bracelet jangled. I didn't feel like I had slept at all.

"What?"

He held the curtain so I could see out. Where we were surrounded by trees the night before, now a field stretched down to some scrub trees and the river. It was early; the sun was just reaching fingers across the field. I heard rustling from the other end of the trailer and Dinah spoke in a husky voice, her face half covered with her blanket.

"Did we do it?"

"Looks like it," Kurt said.

She was immediately fully awake and threw the blanket back.

"Oops. Sorry, Grandma."

Mother opened one eye, and half-glared at Dinah. "What time is it?"

"About 7:00," Kurt said. "I thought we could get into our travel duds and go into town—maybe find a little breakfast and then do some exploring. I'm going to go out and put on the correct license plates while you ladies dress, okay?"

Mother looked at me and grinned. "Is he always this bossy?"

I nodded. "Usually I ignore him, but this time he's right. If we want to get a good look at Route 66, we need to get going."

"Well, I suppose that's the only way I'm going to get any coffee." She looked longingly at the empty stove.

She and I opted for our sundresses while Dinah donned jeans rolled up and a shirt with her saddle shoes from her show choir days. Mother helped her tie a small scarf at her neck and put her hair into a pony tail.

We had put a little water in the tank so that we could use the tiny bathroom. By the time we were done, Kurt was back inside. Mother and I had agreed that we didn't want to spend the day in high heels and instead brought twenty-first century wedgie sandals with us, not all that different from the ones popular in the Fifties.

"I changed out the license plates," he reported. "The road is a little soft. We're lucky we didn't end up sideways in a ditch or something."

"I never thought of that." It gave me a sinking feeling each time I realized the possible results of miscalculation or not considering all of the potential for disaster. But who could? Why did I agree to this? I am not up to the stress of time travel and all of its ramifications any more. I think I hoped that Kurt would come to a better understanding of my previous adventures.

But we were where we were—or *when* we were— time to make the best of it. I reminded myself it was just for one day. And I could tell that Kurt and Mother were really excited about this.

As we prepared to leave, I said, "We need to find some way to mark our spot so we park the camper in the same place when we come back. We don't wake up tomorrow in a treetop or something. "

"You're sure we have to come back here?"

"No, I'm not sure, but I've never done it any other way. Bringing it back to the same spot to make the time change is the only way I'm confident that it'll work."

Dinah said, "Why don't we just leave the camper here? Then we'll know it's in the same spot."

Kurt looked at me. "Maybe that's not such a bad idea. Except we're kind of in the road."

"That and there would be nothing to keep someone from towing it away," I said. "Then we would be in a pickle."

Luckily, we were on the edge of a road but facing away from the town of Times Beach. Turning the rig around did not prove simple. Kurt found a crossroad and I got out and directed until we managed to face the right way.

Times Beach consisted of straight dirt roads lined with small frame houses. A few people were out and watched us pass with no expression. Men in shirt sleeves and trousers—certainly no tee shirts—and women in print house dresses, a few in slacks. There was little to indicate the resort feeling that the town's founders had had in mind. Kurt had to concentrate to keep our rig moving on the soft, slightly muddy, road.

"Hardly conducive to sight-seeing. I'm going to head back toward the Visitor's Center—now a restaurant, I believe."

Sure enough, after we turned on to the main road and neared the river, we spotted the same building we had visited the night before—or sixty-four years later if you want to get picky—but in need of sprucing up. Gone was the crisp gray and white scheme. Instead the once white paint was drab and missing in places. Pots of struggling geraniums spoke of neglect that even the recent rains couldn't remedy. But the parking lot was full-- a good sign in any era. The sign on the roof said 'Steiny's' and a large sign on a pole boasted 'Steaks.' I needed coffee. I am my mother's daughter.

And we were both reassured as we entered and picked up the odor of strong coffee, mixed with that of syrup, bacon, and cinnamon rolls. Waitresses of various ages bustled about with trays to a near-capacity breakfast crowd. One nodded to us as she passed and said, "There're booths open on that side." She indicated with a nod of her head, as her hands were full at the moment.

We didn't get many looks as we headed to the booth —that was a good thing. Dinah looked around while we waited for the waitress.

"It's really noisy."

It was her grandmother who noticed why.

"It's because they're talking to each other, honey. No phones."

I expected her to scoff—she would have if Kurt or I had pointed it out, but instead she slowly scanned the room again. "You're right."

Kurt and I grinned at each other, probably both thinking of times as a child that she came home from school with great revelations like *We're supposed to brush our teeth three times a day!* or *Teacher says we're not supposed to pinch each other.* Great wisdom always sounds better coming from someone other than your parents.

Kurt had arranged to get some contemporary money before we left, and as I looked at the menu, it appeared the day would not cost us much. While we studied our options, an elderly man in overalls and a long-sleeved plaid shirt, despite the warm day, stopped at our table.

"Hey, young lady," he said to Dinah, but glancing at Mother, "Make sure your dad buys you the biggest breakfast on the menu—that would be 'Bruno's Special'."

And he winked at Mother.

Dinah looked startled, and then noticed her grandmother's blush. "Why, thank you, sir. I'll do that."

He moved on, glancing over his shoulder a couple of times.

"Grandma!" Dinah nudged Mother. "He's trying to make a move on you!"

Mother regained her composure and straightened up. "Of course he is. But you realize he's way too old for me. He must be 120 by now."

Dinah giggled as the waitress appeared to take our order. She took the stranger's advice and ordered a Bruno special: scrambled eggs, a thick slice of ham, biscuits and waffles. The food, steaming hot, arrived on thick white china plates. Dinah struggled with the huge meal, so Kurt took the biscuits off her hands. We made it through breakfast and returned to the Jeep.

"What's our plan?" Dinah asked from the back seat.

Kurt put the Jeep in gear and started to pull out. "I'm thinking we'll try and go as far as Cuba and have lunch at the Wagon Wheel Cafe. Then we'll come back to our spot from last night. I want to stop at the Meramec Caverns too."

"Cool," Dinah said.

Traffic on the road had picked up while we were eating breakfast. Dinah gaped at the 'vintage' cars—which of course were actually in their prime. We noticed an abundance of billboards compared to our own time,

41

especially proclaiming the need to visit the Meramec Caverns.

We passed a beautiful log building, the Red Cedar Inn. Kurt said "Maybe we should have waited to get breakfast there."

I noticed the wistful tone of his voice, and said, "Remember, we're trying to keep interaction with the locals at a minimum."

"I know."

The town of Pacific, lined with limestone bluffs, came into view.

"Are those the caves?" Dinah asked, pointing at gaping holes in the bluffs.

"They are caves," Kurt answered, "but from silica mining. They're not the Meramec Caverns."

We continued down the road at slower speeds than we were used to.

"There're so many signs and poles and wires and junk. There're even signs for the caverns painted on barns," Dinah said. "And all of the motels! We don't have that many now, do we?"

"Maybe not," I said. "But the ones we have are bigger and more hidden from the Interstate. You aren't as aware of them as you are when they're right beside a two-lane road."

"Wow! Look at that sign!" Dinah pressed her nose to the window like a kid in a Fifties movie.

The dominant sign for the Gardenway Motel was

partially supported by a glass block base that mimicked the materials used in the motel itself. The name of the motel, outlined by neon, was imposed on a large arrow pointing to the office.

"If I remember right, that one's still open in our time," Kurt said.

"Hope they've done some remodeling by then," Dinah said.

We soon reached Stanton, and the signs advertising Meramec Caverns became more numerous.

"Are we going to stop, Dad?"

"On our way back, if we have time," Kurt said. Lots of signs and business names had a connection to Jesse James, who according to local lore, resided in the area long after his supposed demise. Kurt explained, based on those stories, that James would die this year (1952) in Granby, Texas.

Dinah blew her bangs off her forehead. "He'd be really old."

"About 105," Kurt said.

We continued through Sullivan and Bourbon, a name that gave Dinah the giggles, and began to see signs announcing our approach to Cuba.

CHAPTER SIX

Lynne

A SIGN CONSISTING of wagon wheels welded together announced the Wagon Wheel Cafe, which sat back from the right side of the road. It was built from field stones fitted expertly together and trimmed with white paint. The white daisies and yellow marigolds in the flower boxes showed more care than those we had seen earlier in the day. Kurt pulled in along the side of the gravel parking lot.

We all stretched as we got out. Dinah pointed down a slope behind the cafe at a row of more field stone buildings. "Look! They look like fairy tale cottages."

Kurt put his hand on her shoulder as they both gazed at the pleasant sight. "Those are the motel 'cabins.' I think there's several units in each building."

We turned and traipsed up the slight hill to the cafe's front door. Inside, round tables covered by crisp white cloths surrounded a huge stone fireplace set in the center of the side wall. A passing waitress grabbed a couple of menus from the hostess stand and beamed a smile at us. She wore a white uniform with a red stripe on the collar, down each sleeve, and around the bottom of a flat half-apron.

"Welcome to the Wagon Wheel! Just passing through?" She didn't wait for an answer as she turned and led us to a table near the back.

"Yes, we are," Kurt said to her back.

She whipped the menus onto the table. "Well, glad to have you! Today's special is a hot beef sandwich with whipped potatoes and gravy. One dollar, ninety-nine."

Kurt blurted out, "Homemade whipped potatoes? Not those instant ones?"

The woman let out a guffaw. "Instant whipped potatoes? I wish there were. We peel an awful lot of 'taters at this place everyday."

"Oh." Kurt blushed and glanced sideways at me. "I thought they had something like that."

"Not likely. I guarantee ours started out as real potatoes this mornin', honey."

Kurt tried to regain his equilibrium. "Well, I'll just try them, then! Ladies? What'll you have?"

I squeezed his hand under the table. I knew that he thought he had made a huge blunder, but I had become convinced with the first time trip that comments like that might make people look at you as a little odd, but no one

45

ever thought, *OMG! That person must be from the future!*

"I'm going to have the trout," I said.

Mother folded her menu and handed it back to the waitress. "Me, too."

Dinah wrinkled her nose, not being a fan of fish. "I want the pork chops,—and can I get French fries, please?"

"Sure thing, Darlin', and you probably want a glass of milk with that?" Dinah nodded.

The waitress collected the menus and promised to have their food 'in a jiff.'

Dinah said, "I understand why she calls me 'Darlin' but Dad, she called you 'Honey!'"

My mother laughed. "Dinah, that's just common in the South—and we're nearing southern Missouri. She's not trying to elope with your dad."

"Oh."

Kurt patted her hand, but he still looked pretty abashed over the instant potatoes comment. I tried to distract him by pointing out the knotty-pine paneling and wagon wheel chandelier in the arched open ceiling. Our food soon arrived, and we talked about the sights we had seen that morning, taking care not to drop names or terms that might be overheard and questioned.

The waitress returned to clear the plates. "We have some wonderful apple pie just out of the oven." She winked.

Mother sat back in her chair and wiped her mouth.

"It sounds delicious, but I don't think I could eat another bite."

"Ohhh," I groaned and looked at Kurt. "Do we have time for dessert?"

"Why not? But don't think you're going to sleep all afternoon while I drive." He grinned and ordered the pie a la mode for himself.

Mother pushed back from the table and looked a little pale. "I think I need to lie down for a bit. Do you mind if I go rest in the camper while you do pie?"

"Are you okay?" I asked, alarmed. "Do you want me to go with you?"

"I'll be fine." She got up. "I'm just a little dizzy."

"We can skip pie," Kurt offered.

She insisted we not do that, but, equally stubborn, I insisted on walking out with her, especially since she was dizzy. "Do you have the keys?" I asked Kurt.

He felt in his pocket and muttered, "Think I left them in the Jeep."

"No problem." I put my arm around Mom, and we headed to the door. Outside, she took a deep breath and gently pushed my arm away.

"The fresh air helps." We walked down to the camper and I got the keys out of the ignition to unlock the camper.

"Do you want me to open up the couch?"

"No, no—I'll be just fine. Stop making such a fuss."

I opened a window above the couch anyway to get the air moving.

"Okay, we'll be out soon."

"Go!" She settled back on the throw pillows.

By the time I returned to the table, our warm apple pie with homemade ice cream had arrived and Dinah was devouring strawberry shortcake with real whipped cream. When we finished, Kurt paid the bill while Dinah and I used the restroom.

The souvenirs caught Dinah's eye. As tempting as it was, bringing souvenirs back to our present was another one of those rabbit holes we didn't want to go into. We hurried her along, concerned about getting back to our spot at Times Beach and set up for the night. Kurt tried to herd us once we got outside, but we were looking on down the road to the west to see what we were going to miss by turning back at this point.

"C'mon, girls, it's mid-afternoon. We need to head back. I—Oh, my God."

"What?" I turned back to look at him, and followed his shocked gaze down to where he had parked the car and the trailer. Only there was nothing there.

His voice was a croak. "It's gone."

I searched the end of the parking lot. "Did it roll?"

"No, it's gone. Vanished."

Dinah looked completely confused. "Why would Grandma leave us? Is she okay?" She had told me a few weeks before about a friend's grandmother who was suffering from severe Alzheimer's and how sad it was. I knew that was what was going through her mind.

I tried to reassure her while my mind whirled with worries and questions about what had happened. "She would not leave us. She doesn't even like to back up her Prius and it has a backup camera."

"But then. . ." She frowned and fought back tears.

She was right. The alternative was worse. If Mother didn't drive off with the Jeep and the camper, then somebody else did. And Mother was in it. I brushed my hair back from my face, and my stomach did a few acrobatics. This kind of thing was what I was afraid of when Kurt suggested this gambit. You can't predict what will happen when you time travel. The slightest slip can have huge ramifications.

"I guess we should have left it at Times Beach. And I put the keys back in the ignition. I just figured…" Now I was crying.

"We can't call the cops. You guys don't have proper licenses or anything," Dinah said. I was surprised at her quick grasp of the situation.

I said to Kurt, "What's the worst that can happen if you tell the police you misplaced your license?"

"I'd have to appear in court…oh, wait, not if we find the trailer."

"I don't think we have a choice. We have no way to search for it—we've got to ask for help. Mother's in there."

Kurt nodded but continued to stare at the spot in the parking lot as if the Jeep and camper would reappear. I turned and rushed back to the restaurant. Kurt roused himself, and he and Dinah were on my heels. We all stood clustered forlornly around the door. Our waitress spotted us and came over.

"Did you forget something, honey?"

"No, it's worse than that," Kurt said. "Someone stole our Jeep and camper and my mother-in-law was in it."

"Oh, honey! Are you sure?"

"Very sure. Would you call the police for us?"

She set a tray and rag on the hostess stand and reached for the phone. Dinah looked puzzled as she watched the woman pick up the receiver and speak into it.

"Dorothy, get me the police please. This is Helen at the Wagon Wheel."

Helen relayed the emergency. Kurt thanked her and herded us back to the door. "Let's wait outside."

Kurt paced the parking lot, and ran his fingers through his hair, muttering. He stopped and looked at me, his face full of apology. "What are we going to do if they can't find it?"

I tried to think of anything encouraging — anything remotely hopeful.

"They will find it," I said, with a confidence I didn't feel. "Won't the thieves have some trouble driving that Jeep? Remember they won't be able to put gas in it. And there can't be that many campers like that in this area, can there?"

Kurt shrugged. "You may be right, although I think they can put gas in it. It just wouldn't be very good for it." We stood in silence for a few minutes. Dinah eyed a couple of teenaged boys who went by on bikes and gave me a grin when she caught me watching her. Maybe her previous experiences with time travel gave her more aplomb with this situation. Or, ignorance is bliss.

Finally, an old brown Ford pulled in and a uniformed policeman stepped out. He pushed his cap back on his head.

"You the folks with the stolen car?" He pulled a small notebook out of his back pocket. I noticed a tag over his pocket that said 'Darby.'

"Yes, Officer—our car *and* our camper, with my mother-in-law in it."

"There was a person in the car?"

"The camper," Kurt said impatiently. "She went out to lie down while we finished our lunch."

Darby shook his head. "Okay, I need your name and a description of the vehicles. And your—mother-in-law."

Kurt gave him the information, along with the fact that we were just traveling through from Iowa.

"Could I see your license?"

"Um, that's a problem. I must have left it in the car. Look, can't we get a search going?" Kurt flushed a little. He's not a good liar. The officer gave him a suspicious glance.

I broke in. "I put the keys in the Jeep after I unlocked

the camper for Mom. This is my fault." I choked back a little sob as the guilt hit me full force.

"Do you know the license number?"

"I do." I rattled it off.

"You said it's red? Never heard of a red jeep."

Kurt jumped back in. "We had it painted. It was olive green."

Darby put his notebook back in his pocket. "Where are you going to be?"

"I guess here," Kurt said. "We can't go anywhere. Can you call us if you find something out?"

Darby cocked his head. "Call you? How would I do that?"

Kurt swallowed. "Maybe you could call the restaurant?"

"Be just as easy to come back here." He shook his head as if dealing with a bunch of loonies wasn't easy and got back in his car.

Kurt, Dinah, and I stood there, alone in the parking lot as he drove away. But not as alone as my mother was right now. Was she awake? Would she think that we were driving and she was perfectly safe? How long before the thief discovered her? I pulled Kurt and Dinah into a desperate hug.

I pulled away and wiped my eyes.

"We should go inside, in case he does call. Maybe get some coffee."

"I feel like I should be doing something, but I don't

know what." Kurt led the way back to the restaurant and opened the door. Our waitress was standing right there, still with the tray and the rag. She obviously had been watching us out the window.

"Come in and sit right over there." She indicated a round table by the front window. "Darby's a pretty good cop—I'm sure he'll find it in no time. Would you like something else to eat?"

"Just coffee for me." We followed the waitress to the table. Kurt and Dinah echoed my order.

"You were right," he finally said to me. "There are too many things that can go wrong with time travel. If they don't find that trailer. . ." He couldn't finish

That made me uncomfortable. "Believe me, I would much rather not be right. Anyway, it wasn't just you. Mother wanted to go, too."

A tall, erect woman in a black tailored dress with white piping around the notched collar and the short sleeves, approached our table. Her hair was pulled back with barrettes, and the streaks of gray in her curls probably put her in her late forties or early fifties.

"I'm Arlene Mills," she said. "My husband and I own the cafe and motel. Helen just told me what happened to you folks, and I am so sorry."

"Thank you," I said. "We're hoping the police find it quickly. My mother will be scared to death when she finds out what is going on. She was napping in the trailer when it was taken."

"Oh, how awful! I didn't realize someone was in it. Do you have anyone you need to call?"

"Not really." *Not for fifty or sixty more years.*

Kurt perked up. "Is there a car rental place around here?" I hadn't thought of that but didn't know how we could pay for it anyway. And surely you needed a license to rent a car even in the Fifties.

Arlene shook her head. "St. Louis is probably the closest place. Would you like to use one of the motel cabins to rest in while they look? No charge. I just feel terrible that this happened here." She paused. "Not that it would have been good anywhere, you know."

"I know what you mean. It would be great if we could use a room. For one thing, we don't want to take up your table space all afternoon. If we don't hear from the officer soon." I realized I was already expecting the worst.

"Well, normally we wouldn't care, but we do have to get ready for a wedding rehearsal dinner this evening. I think you would be much more comfortable in a room, too, and maybe could even could get some rest."

I knew we weren't going to rest until that camper was found, but appreciated her thoughtfulness. We left our half-empty mugs and followed her out of the back door of the cafe.

Each stone building that we had noticed earlier appeared to have three or four units in it. Arlene Mills opened the door of an end unit and opened the drapes while we looked around. The room appeared utilitarian but clean. Two beds with green painted metal headboards were covered with white chenille bedspreads. A radiator under one of the windows would provide heat in the cooler months.

"There's some magazines there on the table to help pass the time," Arlene said.

"Thank you so much," I told her. "We really appreciate this."

She promised to let us know as soon as she heard anything, pocketed her keys and left.

I sunk on the edge of the bed and gave way to tears. Kurt came over and patted my shoulder awkwardly.

"Mom, you should lie down for a little bit," Dinah said.

"Don't be so bossy." I couldn't hold back a small smile at her protectiveness. I kicked off my sandals and stretched out on the bed, plumping the pillows a little. Kurt sunk in one of the two easy chairs, and Dinah picked up a copy of *Life* magazine and grabbed the other chair.

The ticking of a windup clock on the nightstand seemed soothing at first but before long increased the level of tension in the room. Finally, Kurt leaned over and turned on the radio, fiddling with the dials until he tuned in some swing music—Glen Miller, maybe. Although I thought there was no way I could sleep, I actually dozed off.

The closing of the door woke me. It took several moments to adjust to the unfamiliar surroundings. Dinah was still sitting in the chair, flipping through a magazine, but Kurt was gone.

She looked at me, sensed my disorientation, and said, "Dad went up to see if there was any news."

I sat up and ran my fingers through my hair. The sinking, hopeless feeling returned. "I'm sure they will let us know."

"I think he just wanted to do something."

I nodded and tried to straighten my dress, smoothing the full skirt as best I could. The fitted waist and snug short jacket were not very comfortable, and now quite wrinkled. Neither the powder blue cotton dress sprigged with daisies nor the white pique jacket were permanent press, that was certain. I went into the little bathroom, washed my face, and tugged a comb through my hair. A college memory came back of getting ready for a blind date who never materialized. I hoped this incident would turn out better.

THE ROMANCE HAD GONE out of the adventure for Dinah as she complained about the lack of TV and phone contact with friends. Several volumes of *Reader's Digest Condensed Books* stood on a shelf over the nightstand. I found a collection of short stories by James Michener that were a sequel to *South Pacific*, one of my all time favorite musicals.

Kurt chose *Signal Thirty-Two* by MacKinley Kantor but couldn't really get into it. He paced, sitting for only a few minutes at a time, during which he opened his book and stared into space. He walked up to the office three times to see if there was any news.

We had the full sympathy of the staff, even though they had no idea how dire the circumstances were for us. I tried to read for awhile, but finally just stretched out on the bed, staring at the ceiling.

What if they couldn't find her? Not only could she be in danger, but she could revert to an infant the next year.

Of course, without the camper, we couldn't get back to our own time. We had no access to funds that would even get us through a week. We had no vehicle and no home. We would have to find jobs, but Kurt's computer and programming skills would be of no use, and my travel agency experience probably wouldn't do me much good either.

I didn't even know how to make a hotel reservation without the Internet. It would be unskilled labor for both of us. Could we even get hired if we had no work record, references, or recognizable Social Security numbers? I was sure we wouldn't starve to death, but it would be a struggle. If our knowledge of the immediate future was more complete, we could play the stock market. But other than a market crash in 1989 and the recession starting in 2008, I certainly didn't have any helpful information at my fingertips. Definitely not for 1952.

And Dinah would have to be enrolled in school in the fall, but how would she be able to fit in, with her knowledge of technology advances, new math, the Beatles and Rap, changes in mores—it was like her first sixteen years had been wiped out.

Of course, none of these concerns held a candle to Mother's safety and what we would do to the future time line by staying in the past. My mind just whirled.

One little ray of hope kept tapping me on the shoulder. The trailer *had* to be somewhere. Even if we had to stay in 1952 for a while, eventually it would have to turn up, wouldn't it?

CHAPTER SEVEN
Linda

I THINK I WAS FIRST aware of a swaying movement, and it seemed to be part of a dream. Then a sudden jerk and bounce brought me fully awake. Apparently Kurt and Lynne decided to let me sleep as we returned to Times Beach. The ride was certainly rougher than it had been in the Jeep, but I didn't know how to let them know that I was awake and to let me out. Surely they would stop soon and check on me.

I hung on to the sides of the couch as I continued to bob and jerk with the movement of the trailer. Dust rolled in the window that Lynne had opened and I managed to pull it closed. As I did, I peered outside.

I didn't recognize the roadside scenery. We were on a gravel road somewhere. What were they doing? Maybe trying to take a different route back for some new vistas? There were small windows in the front of the trailer but because of the vee-shaped front, neither looked directly out at the Jeep.

Moving from one makeshift handhold to another, I made my way to the back and the dinette. I dropped on one of the benches in relief and gripped the table while I peered out the back window. A cloud of dust from the road obscured most of the view, but we were definitely out in the country. We were also traveling at a speed that not only seemed unsafe but also could damage this unique old trailer.

We slowed slightly and then careened to the left around a corner. I was looking out a left side window when the front of the Jeep came into view. It wasn't Kurt driving—or Lynne. That dark curly hair didn't belong to Dinah either. And if they were going to have someone else take this rig somewhere for service or whatever, they would not have left me in it.

That left only one explanation—one that fit the use of back roads and the lack of warning. My driver was a car/camper thief. I fell back on the dinette bench as we hit another pothole and jerked to the right. Whether because of the ride or the realization, my stomach seized and sloshed. I feared I was going to lose that delicious trout I'd had for lunch.

My mind spun with the ramifications. The way this guy was driving, we could easily end up careening down a hillside with me trapped inside. There was a good possibility that my kidnapper didn't know I was back here, but what would he do when he found out? Would he be willing to leave any witnesses? What about Lynne's plan to return to 2016 as quickly as possible? Or if something happened to this trailer, return at all?

There wasn't much I could do while we were moving. I concentrated on a plan for when we stopped. If we were still in the country, I could either hide somewhere—the compartment under the couch—or I could make a run for the woods.

A run seemed like the best bet. If I hid, I would be trapped, with no way to call for help. The camper door was on the opposite side from the driver's door of the Jeep. I couldn't tell when I got that glimpse of the Jeep if there was more than one person in there. Did the thief have a sidekick in the passenger seat who would see me if I ran? Actually, ran is a loose term in my case—I'm sixty-three. But—I realized I had no choice.

I slammed back against the bench as we made a sharp turn and headed uphill. The road continued to wind upward, and I stayed pinned to the bench. My churning stomach was as much due to my regret at urging Lynne to go through with this as it was to the rocky road. She must be ready to kill me. If someone didn't beat her to it.

I tried to get another glimpse of the Jeep's driver or passenger side but no luck. Apparently we reached the top of a hill and began to descend again, requiring a different grip and bracing my feet. The trailer began to slow and came to a rolling stop.

I heard shouting coming from the Jeep but couldn't make out words. I had to be ready; this might be my only chance to get away. I knew it was pretty self-centered but at that moment staying alive trumped all reservations about leaving the trailer with thieves and all the timeline effects involved.

I swung open the door and peered through the window of the door to the Jeep to see if anyone was coming my way. I jumped the short distance to the ground. My right foot slid as I realized too late that a steep slope at the edge of the road led down into a wooded gully.

I grabbed at a nearby branch, slowing my descent but not stopping it. I slid far enough that I could no longer see the Jeep and the camper, and, hopefully, they couldn't see me. I could certainly hear them, though.

Car doors slammed and a woman yelled, "The door came open on the camper!"

"Was there someone in there?" A man.

Pause. The woman: "I don't think so. Maybe it just wasn't latched. You've been driving like a maniac."

"Oh, shut up. Check the camper."

I didn't dare breathe as I listened to the footsteps, the woman, presumably, walking in the camper, and then slamming the door.

"Nobody there. Let's get out of here." A car door slammed.

I slid a little further down the hill, gripping branches

and waited for the sound of the Jeep pulling away. Nothing happened.

Doors slammed again.

"Well, why can't you start it? It was just running." The woman's voice.

The man's voice was muffled from inside the car. I thought I knew the problem. Several years back, cars were changed so that you couldn't start a car without having one foot on the brake. It took me about six months to get used to it. Somehow when he stole the car, he must have accidentally done it right.

I glanced down the hill behind me. If they weren't leaving, I needed to get out of there. A little farther down, the slope was more gradual if I could just work my way to that area.

I located a tree root with one foot, lowered myself and searched for a foothold with the other. Why in the hell did Lynne and I decide to wear dresses and wedgies on this day of all days? My skirt bunched up around my waist and one of my shoes was about to come off— maybe the heel strap was broken. The branch I was gripping snapped with a sound like a shot.

The woman's shrill voice carried down to me again. "I think someone's down there. George, someone was in the camper and they're trying to get away!"

I looked up to see a weathered, middle-aged face peering down at me.

"It's an old lady!" she added. "Should I go after her?"

I couldn't make out George's answer and I wasn't waiting to find out. I let go of the branch I'd grabbed after the other one broke and rolled down to the gentle plateau, hitting several rocks and roots along the way. Every part of my body screamed in pain. As I struggled to my knees. and tugged down my skirt, I heard a voice behind me.

"Lady?" It was a legitimate question. But how could anyone have gotten down the hill any faster than I did? I tried to stand and turn, but my ears buzzed and it felt like flashing lights behind my eyes. I got my balance and turned to face the music — and my captors.

Standing on a rocky ledge behind me were two boys, one about ten or eleven and the other a young teenager. The younger boy wore bib overalls, and a faded blue button-up shirt, and carried a long stick stripped of bark and rubbed smooth. His sandy hair fell over his eyes and he stared with his mouth open, probably at seeing someone his grandmother's age with her skirt upended and slip hanging out.

The older boy had the same color hair, a striped tee shirt, baggy denim pants, and a smirk on his face. Oh, Lord.

I wanted to get these boys to help me, but not put them in any danger. I glanced up the hill. I couldn't see the top but I still hadn't heard the Jeep and camper pull away.

"Boys, I really need help. There's some people up

there who stole our car and trailer when I was in it. What's the fastest way to somewhere I could get help?"

They just stared at me. The younger boy poked the older with his stick. "Frankie," he hissed.

"We don't know you," Frankie said.

"I know, but if you just show me what direction to go?"

The younger boy poked Frankie with his stick again. "We gotta help her," he whispered.

"Quit it, Jerry, or I'll sock you." Frankie sighed. "Okay, follow us." He turned and headed down and to the right to a trail that wound around rocky outcroppings.

I mentally cursed my wedge sandals—certainly not the thing to wear hiking in the woods. I had trouble keeping up. Frankie never looked back, but Jerry, behind me, took pity on my awkward gait and hissed "Frankie, slow down!"

Frankie did, barely. He came to a small ravine and jumped up on a fallen tree that bridged the gap. He put his arms out for balance. Weaving a little, he quickly negotiated the ten or so feet across the log.

I hung back—my balance and coordination had never been great and had deteriorated with age. It wasn't far, but I didn't think I could do it.

Jerry went around me and stepped up on the log, scrambling across with the nimbleness of a squirrel. When he got to the other side, he jumped down, and turned to look at me. He got back up on the log and stretched out the end of his walking stick to me.

"Here. Grab on and don't look down." It was the first thing I'd heard him say out loud.

I reached out and grabbed the end of the stick, and stared Jerry in the eyes. I took a couple of tentative steps. But, if I didn't look down, I would certainly misstep. The log was round, after all. I peeked and the ravine really wasn't very deep. So I watched my feet as I edged along, thinking all the while I would be better off barefoot than wearing these stupid shoes. I stepped off the end of the log and took a deep breath.

Frankie pivoted and continued on, but not before I caught a look of disgust on his face. Well, tough.

"Are you boys brothers?" I asked Jerry.

"Yep."

"I thought as much. You look alike."

Jerry shrugged and plodded on, using his stick to move brush out of the way.

"Are you taking me to your house?"

Jerry shook his head. "We live with our grandma."

"Oh," I said. "Are your parents—never mind. It's none of my business."

The only sound for a few minutes was our thrashing through the brush, and then Frankie said, "Our mom's in jail."

CHAPTER EIGHT
Linda

"I'M SORRY TO HEAR that." A pretty feeble response. "You're lucky to have your grandma." Of course I tend to be sympathetic to grandmas. And a sudden thought gripped me, almost throwing me off-balance: What if I never saw Dinah again?

Frankie said, "Mebbe," and Jerry just ducked his head. A sore spot, then. Of, course, it may just be because they felt their mother had abandoned them.

We reached a gravel road. I had no way of knowing if it was the same one I had traveled in the camper or a different one. I hoped it wasn't the same in case the car thieves were on it.

Neither boy spoke as we trudged along, kicking up dust, until we got to a driveway with a mailbox cantered forward on its post as if was trying to disgorge its mail. A small, unpainted story-and-a-half house slumped along the dirt drive that led back to a tumble-down barn. Nothing about the place encouraged optimism or hope.

Frankie and Jerry slowed down as if reluctant to approach the porch. The screen door creaked open before we stepped up on the uneven surface, and a thin, hawk-faced woman poked her head out.

She gave me the once over and snapped, "What'd you boys do now?"

"Nuthin', Grandma," Frankie whined.

Jerry spoke up, although hesitantly. "This lady needs help."

The woman cackled. "I bet she does." She looked at me. "Whaddya want, money? I ain't got any." She pounded the broom in one hand on the porch floor for emphasis.

"I just need to use a telephone," I said.

"What for?"

I wanted to say *Well, you old bitty, none or your business,* thinking what a depressing place this was for these boys to grow up. No wonder they were sullen and suspicious.

"It ain't long distance, is it?"

I shrugged. "I just need to call the police or the sheriff."

She had turned and started to lead me into the house, but whirled back to face me. "What for? What'd those boys do?"

I held up my hands. This woman was really a piece of

work. "Nothing! They helped me. Someone stole my car. I need to call the police."

"You sure they didn't do it?"

As she spoke, we had entered the house and I began to take in the room I was in. The living room, if that's what it was, was stacked with bundles of newspaper tied up in twine, dog-eared magazines, and cardboard boxes bulging with unknown contents. A narrow path led back to what I presumed was the kitchen door. Brown paper was tacked up over most of the windows.

"No, I know they didn't. It was a man and a woman. He had dark, curly hair."

She looked like she was going to say something else but thought better of it. She put one hand on her hip, the other still holding the broom. From the look of the house, the broom was probably used more as a weapon or a threat than a utensil.

"Well, I don't want no police comin' here."

"I'm sorry," I said. "I don't know what else to do. Is there someone else nearby who could help me?"

"There's a town 'bout two miles down the road. Don't know if you could walk it though, in them shoes."

I smiled. "You're probably right about that. Do you have a car?"

"Got a truck, if you can pay for the gas." She took a stance with both hands on the broom and feet spread apart. It was her last offer.

I felt in the pocket of my dress. "I have two dollars," I

said and held it out.

The woman snatched the bills. "All right, let's go. I got more important things to do." She made a shooing motion, indicating that I should turn around and follow the path back to the door.

Frankie and Jerry, sitting on the edge of the porch, looked up as we came out. The woman said nothing to them but pushed around me and marched across the dirt yard toward a rusty pickup sitting near a ramshackle shed.

Since it appeared that their grandmother wasn't going to explain where we were going, I said, "Your grandma is going to give me a ride to town. Thank you for your help."

They both nodded, and Jerry gave a little wave, as if he didn't want his brother to see it.

I wrestled with the passenger door and climbed up on a dusty, ripped seat. Not that it was going to hurt my outfit. I looked around for a seat belt and realized it was too early for that.

"Now what?" The woman looked at me in disgust.

"Nothing," I said. "I don't even know your name. I'm Linda Marsh." I held out my hand.

She ignored it. "Just Martha. That's all you need to know." She started the truck. I hung on as we bounced out on the pitted driveway and onto the gravel road.

Conversation with Martha was a dead end. She had no interest in me, no curiosity about how I appeared in her life. As we bumped along, I was surprised to notice that the sun was getting lower. I hadn't thought about the time since my abduction, but it had to be late afternoon or early evening. I didn't wear a watch on this part of the trip because of the effect Lynne thought jewelry had on time travel.

"Do you know what time it is?" I asked Martha.

She jerked the steering wheel to miss a small animal on the road and turned to squint at me. "You got some place to be?"

"No...I mean, yes, I'm sure my family's looking for me. The later it gets, the more worried they must be."

Martha huffed, as if that was the most ridiculous thing she had ever heard of. She bent closer to the wheel and peered through the dirty windshield.

"'Bout six, I 'spose," she muttered.

A few minutes later, she suddenly blurted, "You say the guy who stole your car had dark, curly hair?"

"Yes, I think so."

"Kind of a wide flat nose?"

I shrugged. "I don't know. I only got a look through the window when we went around a corner."

"Huh," she said.

We entered the edge of a very small town that appeared to be entirely along the main road. Almost everything looked well-used and not well-taken-care-of. Occasionally a feeble attempt at livening a spot with a pot of flowers or a brightly painted chair relieved the grayness. Two blocks into the town, a gas station and grocery store sat to the right and a bank and dry goods store to the left.

"You can just drop me at the police station," I said.

She laughed a dry, humorless laugh. "No po-lice station here. Sawyers might let you use their phone." She pulled over in front of the grocery and I noticed that in one grubby window, a sign advertised Lucky Strikes and at the bottom said 'Sawyer's Grocery.'

I understood that this was the end of the line for Martha and my two dollars, and I got out of the truck. As I was shutting the door, I tried to thank her but she was already pulling away. I slammed the door quickly to avoid getting dragged along.

I looked down the street and tried to regain some perspective. I wasn't hurtling down the road in a trailer being pulled by thieves. I wasn't stuck in the woods with a couple of sullen boys and their more sullen grandmother. There was surely someone in this town who had a phone and would take pity on me.

On the other hand, I had no idea where I was; I wasn't too sure where I needed to go; and the camper that we needed desperately could be anywhere.

I turned and pushed open the screen door to the grocery. No air conditioning here. No open refrigerated or frozen foods cases blasting cold air in to the aisles. No racks of toys, tee shirts, or magazines. Two aisles of canned goods ended in a meat counter across the back. A wooden check-out counter stood just inside the doors.

A middle-aged, round-faced woman looked up from the heavy metal cash register. "Hi! Can I help you find something?" She smiled, but I could tell she was trying to place me.

I took a deep breath. "I need a phone. Someone stole our car and camper and—"

Her eyes widened. "Really? Right out here?"

I started again. "No, I'm sorry, I'm not making much sense. My daughter and son-in-law—and my granddaughter—we were all having lunch at a cafe. Um, the Wagon Wheel?"

She shook her head. It didn't ring a bell.

"On Route 66. I've forgotten the town. Havana?"

She thought a moment. "You mean Cuba?"

"That's it! I went out to rest in the camper and someone stole the whole rig. I got away not far from here and two boys helped me and took me to their grandmother. I need to get hold of the police and let my family know I'm okay."

"Their grandmother?" she said, still trying to grasp it all. "Martha Swan, who let you out here?"

"She didn't tell me her last name but, yes, her name is Martha."

"But she wasn't the one who stole it?"

"No, she wasn't. They helped me." I could have added, *not willingly*, but didn't. "Is there a phone I can use?"

"Certainly." She left the counter and led me to the

back of the store. A wooden door had a frosted glass window with the word "Office" stenciled in black. A large desk, covered with account books and catalogs, dominated the space. The clerk pulled a black desk phone toward me.

I hesitated. We used dial phones through most of my childhood and I only vaguely remembered the ones requiring an operator for even local calls.

"I don't have the number." I knew 911 would not work.

She looked surprised, but said, "Janice will be able to connect you. The local operator. Just tell her who you want to call."

"I want to call my family, but maybe I should just call the police in Cuba."

"That would be a good start. Actually, you need to call the Crawford County Sheriff. He has jurisdiction here." She was starting to think I was 'a little telched' as my Uncle Bob used to say.

I picked up the phone. The heavy handset felt odd and I almost reached out my hand to dial.

"Operator," came a cheery voice.

"Yes, um, I need to connect with the Crawford County Sheriff...in Missouri."

The dispatcher answered. I gave my disjointed story again. To my surprise, she knew exactly what I was talking about. "Officer Darby from Cuba is on that case. I'll radio him and inform the Sheriff. Where did you say you are?"

"Oh!" I had no idea where I was. "Just a minute." I turned to the clerk. "I don't even know the name of the town I'm in."

She smiled. One could make allowances for an old lady who had been through what I had. "This is Jenkins' Junction. The phone number here is 287-J."

"Thank you." I relayed the information to the dispatcher. She asked about the camper and Jeep and said she would call back as soon as she talked to Officer Darby.

I hung up and turned to the clerk. "Thank you. They're going to call back. My name is Linda, by the way."

She put a hand on my arm. "I'm Phyllis Sawyer. While we're waiting, let's find you a little something to eat. You look all in."

I almost cried.

CHAPTER NINE

Lynne

ABOUT 7:00, there was a knock on the door. Kurt jumped up to answer and opened the door to Officer Darby. He stood there, hands on hips.

"I have some good news. We found your mother-in-law. Actually, she found us."

I rushed to stand beside Kurt. "Is she okay?"

"As far as I know. She turned up at a small town about twenty miles from here—Jenkins' Junction. I'm going to go get her now but wanted you to know."

"Can I ride along?" Kurt asked.

"All of us. Please," I added.

He hesitated, and then said, "Sure. C'mon. The Sheriff is going to meet us there."

Dinah started sobbing and hugged me while I was trying to tug on my sandals.

"Oh, Mom, I was so afraid they wouldn't find her!"

Officer Darby smiled at her. "I think your grandma's one tough cookie, young lady."

Dinah smiled through her tears. "I know she is."

We trooped out to Darby's car. I said to Darby, "You said you found Mother. But not the car and the camper?"

Darby shook his head. "Not yet. Still looking."

Kurt rode in the front and Dinah and I climbed in the back clinging to each other. She finally relaxed a little as we headed out of town.

"This back seat is huge," she whispered to me.

THE ROAD LED into the hills, twisting and turning in roller coaster fashion. Darby explained that he had spoken briefly to my mother and that somehow she had gotten away from the car thieves. She had made it to a grocery store in Jenkins' Junction.

I appreciated the information, but Darby kept turning his head to fill us in as we careened around curves on the narrow road. Made me nervous. We did not need to be in a car accident at this point.

Jenkins' Junction was so small that there wasn't evidence of a junction with anything. Darby pulled up to a small brick building with a weathered wood front. We piled out of the car and rushed into the store.

Loud laughter greeted us. Mother and another woman sat facing each other behind the counter, holding plates with the remains of sandwiches, potato salad, and what looked like to-die-for chocolate cake. The woman was wiping her eyes and choking back laughter at something Mother had said.

Mother had her back to us and, when Dinah threw her arms around her grandmother's neck, nearly jumped out of her chair. She looked up and broke into a broad smile.

"Dinah! You found me!"

"I think you found yourself, Mom." I held my hand out to the other woman. "Hi. I'm her daughter, Lynne. It looks like you've been taking great care of her."

"We've become friends just like that!" She snapped her fingers. "I'm Phyllis Sawyer. My husband and I own this store."

"Well, thank you for everything. I can't wait to hear the whole story."

Mother set her plate on the counter and stood. Her face became serious. "Anything about the camper?"

Officer Darby had been observing the reunion and stepped forward. "Not yet but we will concentrate our search in this area. The county sheriff should be here any minute. I need to get you folks back to the Wagon Wheel."

"Of course," I said.

Mother said goodbye to Phyllis Sawyer and we thanked her profusely.

Kurt gave Mother a hug as we walked out of the store. "Don't scare us like that again. I need you around to keep Lynne in line." He grinned at her.

She smiled too. "Who knew that a simple nap would turn into such an adventure?"

She got in the back seat with Dinah between us. Darby turned the car around to head out of town.

I turned to Mother. "How did you manage to get away?"

"When I woke up, we were on a road like this—" she pointed out the window, "and I soon figured out that you wouldn't be driving that fast, Kurt, and didn't think you would even be on a gravel road. Once when we went around a corner, I got a glimpse of the driver and he had dark, curly hair. Finally they stopped. I decided I had nothing to lose by making a run for it."

She stopped a minute and smirked. "So to speak. Anyway, I opened the door and was so focused on getting away, that I didn't notice that the slope at the edge of the road was pretty steep. Shall we just say that my descent was not very graceful?"

"Oh, Grandma, you mean you fell all the way down the hill?" Dinah said.

"Not all the way—well, yes, pretty much. Anyway, two young boys were at the bottom and took me to their grandmother's house. That was quite an outfit, let me tell you." She described the farm and how the grandmother treated the boys.

"Sounds like Martha Swan," Darby said.

Mother leaned forward. "Yes, I think Phyllis Sawyer said that was the name. Do you know them?"

"I know of them. Every cop in this part of Missouri does. The boys' mother is in prison for robbery and the father should be too, but somehow he got out of it. She wouldn't testify against him—said it was all her doing." He started to brake the car suddenly, and they all jerked forward.

"Ooops. Sorry." He pulled over to the side of the road, stopped and turned around in the seat. "Mrs. Marsh? You said you thought the man who stole your vehicle had dark, curly hair?"

"Yes, I think so."

"That sounds like Martha Swan's son George. The boys' father."

"Oh, dear," Mother said. "Those poor boys. You know, Martha did ask me about that, and if he had a wide, flat nose, but I didn't see him that well."

"Do you have any idea how far it was from your escape to Martha Swan's farm?"

"Nooo. I didn't have my watch on, but I don't think we walked more than an hour—maybe only forty-five minutes or so. And it was pretty slow walking. I don't think it was very far."

Darby picked up the mic for his radio and gave orders to a deputy to meet him at Martha Swan's. He also notified the sheriff of his plan.

As he started the car again, he said, "I would rather take you people back to the Wagon Wheel first, but I'm afraid we might miss an opportunity to catch these guys.

You must all stay in the car — no ifs, ands, or buts. You hear me? Martha Swan and her family are crazy."

"Oh, dear," Mother said again. "Those poor boys."

Darby turned his car around, and we all hung on as we rocketed back toward Jenkins' Junction.

I regretted ever taking seat belts for granted. Before we reached the town, though, he turned onto a steep uphill road. Soon after, he slowed and stopped along the side of the road.

Mother peered out the window at a broken-down farm. "That's the place," she said.

Darby nodded and got out of the car. He swaggered down the drive and up to the porch. He pounded on the door and waited. Finally, a woman came out carrying a broom and nudged him off the porch. They couldn't hear what was being said, but Darby put his hands up, more in protest than fear.

Suddenly, Mother said, "Oh my God!" and pointed toward the trees across from the house. A young man stepped out of the woods holding a rifle. Kurt pushed open his door, yelling and pointing at the same time.

"Darby! Watch out!"

The boy swung the rifle around toward Kurt and my throat closed up. I couldn't speak, but Dinah shouted "Daddy!"

Time seemed to slow down. A single shot pinged Kurt's door and he ducked back in the car, slamming the door behind him.

When I looked back at Darby, he had drawn his revolver and turned toward the boy. The woman swung the broom handle and knocked Darby off the porch. He lay in the dirt not moving, and the old woman stepped down to look at him.

She turned and yelled "Git!" at the boy with the gun, who disappeared back into the woods.

Kurt and I both got out of the car and ran toward Darby, followed by Mother and Dinah. I wanted to tell them to stay put but knew they wouldn't listen.

"You again!" the woman said to Mother as we approached. "I knowed you were nothing but trouble. Told ya I didn't want no cops here."

Kurt held up his hands. "Ma'am, we don't want trouble really. I'll just help Officer Darby to his car and we'll get out of your way."

Darby started to push himself up, shaking his head. "She assaulted me. She—"

A siren split the evening air and another patrol car rolled into the driveway. A very large man in a deputy's uniform got out of his car, his hand on his gun. He rushed to Darby's side and gave him a hand up. I wanted to caution him about possible head injuries, but it was too late.

Darby rubbed his head gingerly. He pointed at Martha Swan and said to the deputy, "Arrest her for assaulting a police officer." He looked at us. "Where'd that boy go?"

"Back into the woods. He took a shot at me and missed," Kurt said, "but I'm afraid he got your car door."

"Won't hurt the runnin' of it," Darby said.

Mother said, "It was Frankie."

"What?" Darby asked.

"The boy with the gun. It's Martha's grandson, Frankie. One of the boys who helped me."

Darby leaned over, hands on his knees, trying to catch his breath. He stood up. The deputy had just finished cuffing Martha Swan and putting her in the back seat of his car. She swore and yelled the whole time. Darby turned to us.

"I gotta go after that boy," he said, apology in his voice. "Can't have a crazy kid roamin' the county with a gun. Then we'll start a search in this area for your trailer and car."

"We understand. But where should we wait?"

Darby hesitated. Dealing with a kidnapping, car theft, assault on an officer, and shooting all at the same time was obviously not in his everyday routine. Another siren in the distance came through the evening air, and Darby smiled. "Sheriff Zuckmayer."

Darby decided that the deputy would return us to the Wagon Wheel, and he would have the sheriff take Martha Swan to the county jail. Darby would organize a search for Frankie and our camper.

It was dark by the time we got back to the Wagon

Wheel and our little unit. Back to waiting. We each tried to read or nap, but weren't successful at either.

Finally, there was a knock at the door. We all jumped up, but Dinah got to the door first and opened it. Darby stood there, hat in hand.

"Nothing yet," he said. "They're watching for it in surrounding towns and we'll be searching more in the morning. You might as well go to bed. Mrs. Mills said you're welcome to stay in this unit tonight."

Kurt's shoulders slumped. "Thank you for your efforts. It's just—we have no where else to turn. This is our whole family—," he indicated the room, "and we really don't have any close friends that we could ask for help." A commentary that made us look pretty pathetic, but there was no alternative explanation that would be acceptable.

"I'm hopeful we'll get a sighting once it's daylight. Don't give up. We've notified all of the area agencies." He gave a faint smile.

"How's your head?" Mother asked.

He rubbed it. "Okay. I guess I'm too hard-headed to do much damage. Good night."

"Good night, and thank you again."

When the officer was gone, Kurt dropped in the chair and put his head in his hands. "This was such a bad idea."

Mother patted him on the shoulder. "It was me as much as you."

"Who could have guessed this would happen?" I said. "Don't beat yourself up about it. Think about it—they can't go far. Once they run out of gas, they're stuck."

He looked up. "You were afraid of something like this. I should have listened."

Dinah just sat, her face drawn and worried.

"I suggest we try and get some sleep," I said. "I guess it's undies so we don't look any worse tomorrow. Something good will happen—I just feel it."

Kurt saw through my bravado—I could tell from the look on his face—but he just nodded and got up.

We were soon in bed. None of us could concentrate on reading and, with no TV, games, or anything else, it seemed the wisest choice.

CHAPTER TEN

Lynne

I WOKE UP the next morning while it was still dark, and lay there mulling over the possibilities. Nothing had changed since the night before. No new brilliant ideas had sprung to mind. We were at the mercy of the authorities or some stranger finding our trailer and Jeep. Then I had a more jarring thought. What if the people who stole it decided to sleep in it? Would they then disappear into some other time period along with the camper?

As the saying goes, and I find it to be true, things are darkest before the dawn. Problems seem magnified to me in those very early, dark hours. I projected all sorts of frightening scenarios — none of which landed us back safe and sound in our own time.

Then I remembered a quote by author Cheryl Strayed that I had just read a few days before. *Fear, to a great extent, is born of a story we tell ourselves, and so I chose to tell myself a different story.* Maybe I should try positive thinking for a change—not my strong suit, but we needed a different story.

I thought of my words to Kurt the night before. The thieves would definitely be limited in how far they could get.

Even if we never found it, our whole family was together. Of course, there was still the issue of what would happen the next year—Mother's birth year. And then how would that affect her and her real parents living in our home? And the timeline?

Don't think about that! The thieves couldn't get gas. At least I didn't think so. *Hang on to that thought.*

My head hurt. I felt Kurt stirring and heard his early-morning husky voice. "What time is it?"

I held up my watch to the beam from an outdoor light coming through a parting in the drapes. "5:30."

Kurt raised up on his elbows and looked around. "Ohhh," he groaned. He dropped back on his pillow.

"Yeah."

He covered his face with both of his hands and muttered through his fingers, "I was hoping it was a dream."

"I know. It's not. Never have I needed coffee so much."

He got up, padded around to the front door, and peeked through the curtains. "There are lights on in the cafe," he whispered. "I'll go see if I can get us a couple of cups. I doubt if this free room includes room service."

"Better put some pants on," I said.

"Right." He took his clothes into the tiny bathroom, so he could turn on the light. Soon he was back out. "I guess motels don't provide toiletries yet. I'll ask when I'm up there if there's somewhere nearby I can get toothbrushes and toothpaste."

"That would be great."

While he was gone, I got up as quietly as I could and took my own clothes into the bathroom. My hair was the biggest challenge, but I managed to get it looking less like a fright wig. It occurred to me that in 2016, almost anything goes in appearance, and few outfits or hairstyles cause heads to turn. Not true in the 1950s.

When I came out of the bathroom, Kurt wasn't back, but my mother was stirring. I filled her in on Kurt's errand.

All she could say was, "Yes. Coffee."

By the time Kurt returned, we were dressed and milling around restlessly. He carried a tray with four steaming ceramic mugs of coffee—no Styrofoam around yet—plus a small white paper sack.

"There's a drugstore just down the block." He handed me the sack, and I pulled four toothbrushes and a tube of Ipana out.

"Bucky Beaver?" I grinned.

"Who's Bucky Beaver?" Dinah stifled a yawn.

"Advertising gimmick for this toothpaste. I'm first." My mouth felt like the inside of a garbage disposal, and I was beyond being polite.

After we had all cleaned our teeth and freshened our breath, Kurt said, "The cafe is open. Are you all ready for some breakfast?"

"I'm starved," Dinah said. "Let's go!"

"You are always starved." We went out the door.

IF NOT FOR THE virtual axe hanging over our heads, breakfast would have been delightful. The smells of sausage and waffles cooking, the cheerful but not annoying clatter of dishes and silverware, and wonderful homemade taste of everything was a treat for the senses. Nearby conversations centered around the upcoming Summer Olympics in Helsinki, Finland and Bob Mathias' chances of repeating his decathlon title.

One woman at another table told her companions about a new book she was reading, *The Diary of a Young Girl* by someone named Anne Frank. "It's a true story and very sad, but amazing too. Those Nazis can't be punished enough."

"They'll never find 'em all," a man at the same table said.

At another table, more somber voices speculated on the polio epidemic. I recalled that 1952 was the worst year and it made me shudder. An older woman said, "You know Ruby Sterns, don't you? Their daughter came home from playing with a friend and complained of a stiff neck. She called the doctor immediately and next thing you know, they were taking her up to Sister Kenny's in Minneapolis. Supposed to be the best place."

We were finishing up our plates of eggs, sausage and pancakes when Officer Darby appeared behind Kurt's chair.

"Don't want to interrupt your breakfast, but I think we found it." His voice was soft, but pleased.

"What?" Kurt's head snapped around. "Really? That's wonderful news!" He pushed his chair back, nearly running over the policeman, and stood up, reaching out to shake Darby's hand. "Where is it?"

"That's the problem. Not too far—about five miles from Martha Swan's place—but we couldn't get your jeep started. There's something wrong with it."

"The keys were still in it?"

Darby nodded. Mother reached out and grabbed Dinah's and my hands, squeezing them tight. Her grin went from ear to ear.

"That's a relief. It's kind of quirky—I think I can get it going." Kurt's voice was ebullient.

"Is that thing a custom job? The dash is kind of strange," Darby said.

"Uh, yeah, it is. My brother-in-law did it."

"Well, as soon as you finish, I'll give you a ride to it and we'll see if we can't get you back on the road."

"We're finished," Kurt said, and then looked at the

rest of us. "Aren't we?"

We all nodded, we were so eager to get this nightmare over. Kurt paid the bill and we trooped out to Darby's car. He looked at us doubtfully.

"Are you sure you all want to go? We could come back and pick you up."

"I think at this point we just want to stay together," I said.

Mother and Dinah agreed.

Darby ushered us into the back seat and Kurt took shotgun. Other than a city emblem on outside, nothing set this car apart from others. Thankfully, no cage separated us from the front. We didn't need any more stress at this point, no matter how minor.

Once in the car, Kurt asked Darby, "Did you catch the guy who took it?"

Darby shook his head. "They were long gone. I suspect it was Martha Swan's son and his current girlfriend. We'll see when we catch up to him."

Mother leaned forward. "What about Frankie?"

"We got him," Darby said. He shook his head. "He's headed for Boonville."

"What's Boonville?" Dinah asked.

"Boys' training school. They'll whip him in to shape."

Mother shuddered. "I don't think those boys ever stood a chance."

"Prob'ly not," Darby said, but didn't seem overly concerned.

The Jeep and camper rested along a gravel road about a twenty-five minute ride from the restaurant. Kurt and I checked out the Jeep and then the camper. No one was inside and no sign of any damage. Kurt got into the driver's seat of the Jeep while Darby leaned over the open door. The Jeep started right up.

Darby scratched his head. "How'd you do that?"

Kurt indicated his feet. "You have to put the brake on before you shift into drive. It's a little-uh-safety thing that my brother-in-law added."

"What are them extra buttons on your key thing, there?"

"Remote locks." Kurt clicked the remote twice to lock and reopen the doors. "Also my brother-in-law."

"Well, I'll be. He should patent that. D'ya want me to follow you back to the highway?"

"That would be great. Thanks for all your help. We'll go back to the Wagon Wheel before we head out, to straighten up our room and thank them as well."

Mother, Dinah, and I had already secured our seats in the Jeep, like we were afraid it would vanish without us if we didn't.

Once we were moving along the gravel, I said to Kurt, "I'd like to meet this clever brother-in-law of yours. What do you think happened? Why did they abandon it?"

"I think it was probably the same problem Darby had. They stopped here for some reason—maybe to take a leak or something—and couldn't restart it."

"They were having trouble starting it when I got away, but this isn't the same place. They must have accidentally got it right," Mother said.

"Do we still have gas?"

"Yup—plus the extra can back in the camper." He smiled—the relief lighting up his face. "We're going to go back to Times Beach to our spot and we are not leaving this rig the rest of today."

"No more sightseeing on Route 66?"

"Not unless we can see it from the windows."

Dinah leaned forward, her earlier fears apparently forgotten. "We don't get to go to the caves?"

"They're still around in 2016. We'll go tomorrow," Kurt said.

"Okay." But there was a little pout.

WE STOPPED BACK at the Wagon Wheel, thanked Arlene Mills and our waitress Helen, picked up our toothbrushes from the cabin, and headed back east. We retraced our route of the day before, opting for sandwiches in the camper rather than any of the lunch stops. We took turns using gas station restrooms so as not to leave our vehicles alone. We were all paranoid.

It was early afternoon when we bounced down the rutted road where we had parked two nights before. It took a couple of back-and-forths before Kurt found the string he had tied on the bush and was satisfied that we were parked in the same spot. The gas gauge was getting low. We settled in for a long afternoon.

We each had our own books. Mother and Dinah played several games of rummy. By mid afternoon, heavy dark clouds had moved in and thunder rattled the windows. Dinah looked out the window with concern.

"What if it rains so hard, the trailer gets stuck here?"

"We would only be stuck if it was also raining in 2016," Kurt said.

"Or we get blown away in a tornado." Dinah wasn't letting go.

Mother leaned over and covered her hand. "Honey, it's going to be okay. Please relax."

"I know, Grandma, it's just..." She shook her head and tears inched down her cheeks. My heart broke as I went to put my arm around her. What were we doing to her?

"The worst is over." I hoped that was true. "We have Grandma and the camper back, and tomorrow we'll be back to normal." I smiled at her. "As normal as we get anyway." I knew she was having a reaction to the stress of the last twenty-four hours.

"I'm sorry, Mom," she mumbled into my shoulder.

Kurt stood by looking helpless. "Hey, Minnie Mouse." He used the pet name he had called her when she was a little girl. "How about if I unhook the Jeep, and you and me will go see if we can find some ice cream?"

Dinah sat up straight and dried her tears. "Thanks,

Dad, but I'm not a little kid. I'll be fine in a minute—it just kind of got to me, the rain and everything." She got up from the bench and kissed him on the cheek. "Besides, you don't want to unhook the Jeep in this mess."

He agreed, rather sheepishly and turned back to his book.

"Why don't you and Mom play cards with us?" Dinah asked.

"Good idea," he said. We all squeezed in to the little dinette. The next couple of hours went more quickly with a couple of games of Liverpool rummy.

The storm caused a slight rocking of the little trailer, but we were cozy and having a good time. The battery kept the lights on until we were ready to call it a night and hopefully move to a different decade and century.

CHAPTER ELEVEN

Lynne

BUT IT WAS NOT to be. I awoke the next morning to the patter of light rain on the camper roof. I lay there hoping that meant that there was a similar weather pattern in 2016 as 1952. But when I peeked through the curtains, I was dismayed to see the same desolate roadside and no rows of pines and hardwoods surrounding us.

My heart was engulfed with dismay. What had gone wrong? As I sat staring out the window, my restlessness woke Kurt.

"What is it?" he said.

I turned to him. "We're still in 1952."

"What?!?" He sat up so fast, he hit me in the head with his elbow.

"Ow!"

"Sorry. But I hoped you were kidding." He leaned over me to look out the window.

"I wish I was."

"What happened?"

"I don't know." Now I was practically in tears. And Dinah was not going to take this well.

I pulled my knees up and rested my head on my arms in defeat. As I did, the coin bracelet jingled.

"Oh my God." I lifted my head and staring at the piece of cheap jewelry. "I forgot to take the bracelet off."

Kurt immediately brightened. "But that's great! I mean, at least we know what went wrong. All we have to do is make it through another day and make the change tonight."

I was somewhat relieved, but totally disgusted that such a careless oversight condemned us to twenty-four hours more of uncertainty and worry.

"I guess. But how stupid of me! I know better."

Kurt put his arm around me. "We were all exhausted. It was such a stressful couple of days. Don't beat yourself up."

"We're about out of food and water, and the battery's almost dead, I'm afraid."

"We'll deal with it. I'm going to get dressed and scope things out—see if we're buried in mud. But since we aren't going anywhere, it really doesn't matter."

"I hope not."

He slid off the bed and pulled his rather wrinkled pleated pants and shirt on and smoothed his hair. He found a windbreaker, since it was still raining.

I got up too and lit the stove under the prepared coffee pot. Mother (and probably Dinah) were going to need something to bolster them when we gave them the news. Fortunately they seemed to be sleeping well, and under the circumstances, there was no reason to wake them since we weren't going anywhere.

Once dressed, I filled two chipped mugs with coffee and carried them outside. Kurt accepted one and frowned as he looked over the fields.

"What are you doing?"

"I just checked the tires—we've sunk a little but not bad. It's so peaceful out here, if you don't think about being in the wrong time and the pollution going on around us that hasn't been discovered yet and a lack of food and. . ." He stopped and screwed up his face. "Well, peaceful anyway."

I stuck my arm through his. "We'll get through this," I said, with more conviction than I felt. "How much money do you have left?"

He stuck his hand in his pocket and pulled out a roll of bills and some change.

"A little over $20. We could get a big breakfast and a few groceries for supper."

I looked at the camper tires dubiously. "You think we can pull that out of here? And do we want to go to a restaurant and take a risk of someone stealing it again while we're inside?"

"You're right. We'll just find a store. I don't suppose

we can buy bottled water, but maybe we can find some place to refill a jug or two. And yes, I think we can pull the camper out."

The camper door opened. "Mom? Dad?"

"Over here, honey," Kurt said.

Dinah came down the steps wrapped in a small quilt. "We're still here."

I held up my wrist. I thought about making a joke about it but didn't. "I forgot to take this off." I did now and dropped it in the mud.

"We have to stay another whole day?"

I didn't remind her that I wasn't the one who wanted to take this detour. "I know—under the circumstances, twenty-four hours seems like a long time, but we'll make it. Let's see if we can scare up something for breakfast."

The expression on her face told me she wasn't fooled by my attempt to be cheerful.

When I followed Dinah inside, Mother was sitting on the edge of the dinette bed looking forlorn. "It didn't work," was all she said. It wasn't accusing, just despondent.

I explained about the bracelet and reminded her that every time we had used the trailer previously, we had been successful in our return. She brightened a little.

"We need to come up with some food. Kurt thinks it isn't too muddy to pull the trailer out and we'll find a store where we can pick up a few necessities. Meanwhile, I do have a dozen eggs in the fridge and we've got a few pieces of bread left to make some toast."

"Then I'd better get dressed and Dinah can help me put this bed back."

I hugged her. "You're amazing, Mom. You're the only one of us who hasn't made a trip before and you're so trusting."

"Not much choice, is there?" There was a little catch in her voice in spite of her smile. She shook out her crumpled sundress, "This probably isn't up to the current grooming codes. You don't have an iron in here, do you?"

"Sorry."

We busied ourselves to make the time go faster. I stirred up some scrambled eggs and Dinah showed her grandmother how to make toast in the relic with drop down sides that we had picked up at the secondhand store. Mother pretended she hadn't seen one before.

Kurt got out some paper plates and plastic forks, since we didn't have much water to wash dishes with. We bumped into one another, all trying to pretend that this wasn't getting us down. Finally, we sat down, toasted each other with fresh cups of coffee and dug in.

Kurt explained to Mother and Dinah how we would take the camper with us to locate a store and then return to this spot to make our transition through time that night. We hoped.

He didn't say that, but I'm sure we all thought it.

We were just finishing up when there was a loud knock on the door, causing us all to jump.

"Who is that?" Dinah said.

Kurt got up. "I guess we'll have to answer to find out." He glanced around the camper to make sure there wasn't any 2016 evidence lying about and then opened the door.

A large man wearing a Stetson peered up at him.

"Sir. I'm Sheriff Phil Barney. Will you step outside, please?" Despite his size, his voice was a little high.

"Sure," Kurt said, as he descended the steps. "What is this about?"

Meanwhile, Mother mouthed 'Barney Fife?' and giggled. Dinah didn't get it, but I shushed her so we could hear the conversation from outside.

"Is this your car and trailer?" the sheriff was asking Kurt.

"Yes, it is."

"Can I see some registration?"

"I'm sorry, I don't have it with me. Why is it necessary?"

I jumped up from the table and hurried out to stand by Kurt.

"Ya see, sir, this trailer and Jeep were reported stolen a couple days ago over in the next county. If you can't show me proof of ownership, you're going to have to come with me."

"But, I was the one who reported it stolen — to, um, Officer Darby in Cuba. He found it yesterday."

The sheriff pushed his hat back. "I haven't been

notified about that, and, seein's as you're a stranger, don't think I'll take your word for it. You need to come along with me."

"But. . ." Kurt looked at me, frightened. What else could go wrong?

"Honey," I said, "we'll get it straightened out. You better leave me some money 'cause we've gotta get Mom's heart medicine." I winked at him—just a feeble attempt to play on the sheriff's sympathy. He wasn't impressed but Kurt pulled the small wad of bills out of his pocket and handed them to me.

The sheriff turned to me. "You got a brother or daddy who can help you out of this mess, little lady? I'll have one of my deputies come and haul this rig to the station."

I seethed but said, "Why, shore, Sheriff. But my husband's innocent." He ignored, or didn't recognize, my fake attempt at hillbilly.

"We'll see. Better get a law-yer." He took Kurt's arm and led him to his patrol car.

As soon as they took off, I rushed back into the trailer. "He's arresting Kurt for stealing our own camper! Help me get things put away—we need to get to the station."

Mother started putting things away. "Gonna call your daddy or brother, little lady?"

"I nearly threw my eggs at him. I'm not letting anyone else drive this anywhere."

We soon were all three in the Jeep and I put it in four-wheel drive. For a few seconds, it seemed like we might not be going anywhere, but gradually the wheels took hold and we began to move forward. Dinah cheered and she gave Mom a high five.

Then she leaned forward to my seat and said, "Are we going to be like that Thelma and Louise movie you made me watch?"

"Made you watch? Right!"

I found the road that would lead us back into town. I stopped when I saw a woman putting a letter in her mailbox and swiveling the red flag up. She looked up and smiled, and I asked for directions to the sheriff's office.

When I pulled up in front of the little white clapboard building, two deputies coming down the steps glanced at us and then did a double take. Little lady, indeed.

As the three of us marched up the steps, the deputies waited for us.

"Is that the stolen camper?" a young, thin one asked.

"Not any more," I said. "It belongs to us. It was stolen Tuesday and we just got it back yesterday."

"Well, the sheriff just brought the thief in," the deputy said.

"No, that's my husband."

The deputies rolled their eyes at each other and moved aside. The shorter, heavier one pointed up the steps. "You better talk to the sheriff. That unit isn't going anywhere until we get this straightened out." They moved down the stairs to stand guard over our camper. I wasn't worried—I had the keys.

We walked into a small, utilitarian reception area. A middle-aged woman with glasses perched low on her nose looked up from behind a high wooden counter.

"May I help you?"

"The sheriff just brought my husband in here?"

"Well, he brought someone in." She examined my mother and Dinah behind me. "Are you all together?"

"Yes. Can we join my—"

"You'll have to wait out here." She nodded toward several scarred wooden arm chairs lined against the wall. We sat. I felt like I was waiting to go in the principal's office.

Dinah nudged me and pointed discreetly at two drinking fountains on the opposite wall. Above the larger one was a sign that said "Whites only" and above the other the sign stated "Coloreds only."

"Look at that," she whispered.

"Jim Crow laws are still in effect. We'll talk about it later." I noticed the receptionist eying us. Dinah frowned at the woman.

"There's some magazines on the table in the corner," said the woman. Apparently she wanted us busy.

"Thank you." I went over and picked up a *Ladies' Home Journal* and took it back to my chair. Dinah looked over my shoulder as I leafed through it. "No giggling," I said out of the corner of my mouth. She smirked.

Mother leaned her head against the wall and soon dozed off, waking every few minutes and looking around bewildered. At times, I could hear raised voices coming from the back office. I wasn't sure that Kurt was one of them. Flies buzzed around the open window and the wait gave me time to notice the overall grubbiness of the place. I was thinking Mom probably shouldn't be leaning against the wall with its dirty light green paint, when the outside door opened and a young boy came in. He was dressed in bib overalls and a plaid shirt and was shoeless. A small dog trailed him in.

The receptionist looked up and sighed. "What is it this time, Eddy?"

"I need to talk to the Sheriff. Someone stole my bike!"

"You said that last week, and then you remembered where you left it." She continued stapling stacks of papers and filing them.

"No, really! This time I left it in front of the drugstore, and when I came out, it was gone!"

"Well, the Sheriff is busy."

"But this is 'portant!" he whined.

"It always is."

A door in the back corner opened and Kurt came out, followed by the sheriff. Kurt shook his head at me, and his red face didn't bode well for a positive resolution.

The sheriff headed for the counter. If anything, his face was redder than Kurt's.

"Patsy, get the sheriff's office over in Crawford County on the phone for me." He turned to Kurt. "Just sit over there with your family, if that's who they are, and don't even think about leaving."

"Kurt, what's going on?" I pulled him down in an empty chair beside me.

He whispered to us, glancing up frequently at the receptionist. "We can't prove it's ours. Well, we can, but our registration says 2016. I'm not going to show them that. What are we going to do?"

His defeatism affected me more than any of the events of the last two days. Usually he blustered through, whether he knew the answer or not.

The sheriff's call was put through, but it was difficult to hear everything he was saying or to interpret which way the full conversation was going. There was an undertone of argument. Finally, the sheriff slammed the phone down.

Patsy raised her eyebrows.

"He's coming over to pick up the camper. And the prisoner. Thinks they've got prior jurisdiction." His tone said he didn't agree, but he turned to Kurt. "Come with me." He grabbed Kurt's arm and half dragged him down a short hallway.

"Wait!" I called and jumped up from my chair. "Where are you taking him?"

The slam of a cell door was my answer.

CHAPTER TWELVE

Lynne

DINAH LOOKED AT ME with panic written all over her face. "Mom! He's locking Dad up!"

I felt the same panic, but knew I had to hold it together for Dinah's and Mother's sakes.

"Surely when Sheriff Zuckmayer gets here, we'll get this straightened out." I wished I felt that confident. I turned to Patsy. "How long will it take the sheriff to get here?"

"About an hour unless he has lunch first."

Lunch. Much as I hated to leave Kurt in that cell, lunch would give Mom and Dinah something else to think about.

"Is there somewhere nearby where we could get something to eat?"

"There's Bill's across the street." Then she looked at us as if seeing us for the first time. "I'm sorry for your troubles."

"Thank you." She probably meant that she was sorry we gotten hooked up with a crook, rather than being sorry that we were trapped in the wrong time period and had become victims of the system without current ID and papers.

The little cafe across the street offered large windows from which we could watch for the arrival of Sheriff Zuckmayer. I wasn't sure what to expect from that turn of events but hoped it would all be straightened out. I couldn't figure out, though, why Sheriff Zuckmayer didn't tell Patsy that the trailer had been recovered and returned to us. Would Kurt just be moved from one jail to another?

Mother brought that up as soon as we sat down. "Do you think they're going to let Kurt go? If not, what will we do?"

"We could break him out of jail and then just hide out until night," Dinah said.

I frowned at her as I noticed the waitress coming up behind her. We ordered BLTs on toast and iced tea. The waitress left, and I said, "Honey, we're not the James Gang."

"I know." She twisted a lock of hair around a finger.

But I considered it. Might there be a time when he was being transferred that he could escape? We had to keep possession of the camper at the same time. Who would drive the Jeep and trailer back to Crawford County? Would they let me do that? It seemed like I had spent the last two days asking myself questions for which I had no answers.

One bright spot was that the sandwiches were excellent. The lettuce was crisp, the tomatoes deep red and juicy, and the bacon probably came from a local farm.

"Mmmm." Mother used her napkin to neatly swipe a glob of mayo from her chin. "I don't think I've had a tomato this good in years. I feel guilty having something so delicious while Kurt sits in a cell."

"I know," I said, "But he will understand. This is just such a mess."

She and Dinah both nodded, and that was the end of any conversation. We were only about half done when I saw Sheriff Zuckmayer's car pull up. He took the steps to the sheriff's office two at a time. I handed Mother some money and said, "Will you take care of the bill?" I got up from my chair. "I think I'd better get back there and find out what's going to happen."

Mother said, "Of course." And she left half of that beautiful sandwich and headed to the cash register.

"You stay with Grandma and come as soon as you can," I said to Dinah and hurried out the door.

Sheriff Zuckmayer was talking to Patsy when I got back inside.

"Why would he leave for lunch? I told him I was coming right over."

"He should be back any time, but you just need to sign for the prisoner and then you can take him. What about the vehicles? And the family?" Patsy pushed some papers in front of him, pulled a pencil out of her hair, and handed it to him. He looked at it, shook his head, and scratched his name on the paper.

"Family?"

Patsy pointed at me as I stood behind him. "But didn't you bring a deputy to take the car and trailer back?"

Zuckmayer whirled around to face me. "And you are...?"

We had left the Swan farm before the sheriff arrived. Of course he would not recognize us.

"Lynne McBriar. This is all a misunderstanding. The Jeep and the camper belong to us. It's my husband that they put in jail. He's not the thief."

He looked from us to Patsy. "Darby never notified me that the property had been recovered." His tone was skeptical. "Let me use your phone," he said to Patsy.

He stared up at the ceiling while he waited for someone to answer.

"Frank Darby, please." Pause. "He what?" He shook his head. "Have him radio me. It's Sheriff Zuckmayer."

He hung up and turned around. "He's home sick today. Seems Martha Swan clocked him a good one the other night. I can't waste any more time here. Can you drive that thing?" He pointed at me.

"Sheriff, it's stolen property," Patsy protested.

Thanks, Patsy.

"She's not going anywhere else if I have her husband, right?" He looked at me. "Can you drive it or should I have it impounded here?"

"No! I mean, I can drive it. We don't want to stay here." I could hear the panic in my voice.

The door opened and Dinah and Mother came in. They hurried to my side.

"What's happening, Mom?" Dinah had the same fear in her voice. I looked at the sheriff.

He sighed. "I'm taking your father back to Cuba in my car and your mother will drive the trailer."

"Thank you," I breathed.

"I will go first and you follow me. No turns or detours, y'hear?"

"Yessir."

A deputy brought Kurt out from the cells in handcuffs. Zuckmayer briefly explained what was happening and ushered us all out the door.

Another deputy sat on the steps outside watching the camper. The sheriff put Kurt in the back seat of his car and I unlocked the Jeep so we could get in. We skipped the seat belts for fear it would raise more questions. Thank goodness I had Kurt show me how to disconnect the warning beep before we time traveled.

Again we followed Route 66 to Cuba. Once we were on the highway, we buckled up.

"Do you know what's happening, Lynne?" Mother asked.

I shook my head. "Apparently Darby's feeling the after effects of his knock on the head the other night—he didn't notify the sheriff that the camper had been found and returned to us. And he's home sick today. Hopefully he'll return the sheriff's call and get this straightened out."

"Wow. We can't catch a break, can we?"

I concentrated on the road. We passed the same roadhouses and motels, the same billboards for the Meramec Caverns. The bluffs and the river were beautiful, but they were lost on us. Dinah hung over the seat but was uncharacteristically quiet.

"Are you okay, honey?"

"Yeah—I think. I promise I will never suggest we do this time travel again."

Mother patted her hand. "It wasn't just you, Dinah. Everybody but your mom thought it was a good idea."

"Don't worry about it. What's done is done. We should have brought fake IDs and registration, but too late now. We *will* get out of this." I was getting good at this confidence thing.

When we arrived in Cuba, we passed the Wagon Wheel Cafe and continued into downtown Cuba. The sheriff pulled in in front of a small brick building with a sign that said 'Cuba City Police.' He motioned to me to pull into the alley alongside the building. We got out of the Jeep and walked around the corner to find the sheriff getting Kurt out of his car. To our surprise, he turned and smiled at us.

"Well, you people seem to get yourselves in one scrape after another. But Darby radioed and vouched for you. He thinks George Swan is the thief."

"It's not been a good couple of days. What happens now?"

"I suggest you go on your way—and don't go back to Times Beach."

That was a problem, but at that point I didn't want to look a gift horse in the mouth.

The sheriff proceeded to remove the cuffs from Kurt's wrists.

"But—?" Kurt started and then shut his mouth.

"Sheriff Barney gets a little carried away with his authority," Zuckmayer said. "I didn't want to argue with him, or he might not have turned you over to me, but it is our jurisdiction. Darby's a good officer, and I'll take his word for it that you're the rightful owners. He said you don't have any registration?" Now he looked like he was rethinking his decision.

Kurt shook his head. "I cleaned out the glove box before our trip and accidentally left it home."

"Well...get going before I change my mind."

"Thank you," I said.

Mother walked over to him. "Can I give you a hug?"

Zuckmayer blushed and gingerly submitted to her exuberance.

ONCE WE WERE all back in the Jeep, I leaned over and clutched Kurt. "I was so worried." I felt tears come to my eyes.

"You and me both. But now what? He said not to go back to Times Beach?" He started the Jeep and looked at me for direction.

"I wish I knew. We don't know for sure that the camper has to be in the same place to change time. I've never needed to try it, and I never asked Ben about it. What do you think about continuing west as long as we have gas and trying to make the time change tonight wherever we are? If it doesn't work, we can go back to Times Beach tomorrow and take our chances."

Kurt thought a moment. "But if we have to go back tomorrow, we might not have enough gas. I guess we could try putting leaded gas in if it was either that or not getting back to our time."

"What could happen? I don't even know."

"I doubt if one tank or less would do much damage. I don't really know."

Mother piped up from the back seat. "If it ruins the Jeep, I'll buy you a new one." She paused and grinned. "Or maybe a good used one."

"I'll help," Dinah added.

We laughed, for the first time all day, and Kurt put the car in gear. "All right, let's go for it!" Then he looked at me. "Are you okay with that?"

I took a deep breath. "Sure. How could I turn down a new car from Mom and Dinah?"

We headed out of Cuba to the west. It was getting well past mid-afternoon so I pulled out the map to look for a destination. The map was dated 2015.

"When you pass a gas station, stop and see if we can get a map current for this year or last. I think they still give them away."

"Good idea."

There were stations all along the route, and it didn't take long to procure a 'new' map. Kurt had brought along a little reference book which handily listed old sites that still existed in 2016, and I went back and forth between the map and book.

"Here's a possibility about thirty miles down the road. 'John's Modern Cabins' was operating in the Fifties but abandoned when the route moved and is now just ruins. But at least it's still there. Maybe we could pay them to stay in their parking lot; that way we would know that nothing new would built over our parking spot. And if we do have to go back to Times Beach, it won't be terribly far."

Kurt nodded. "We'll check it out."

The narrow road took us past St. James and around the west edge of downtown Rolla. We began to relax enough to take in the quaint sights along the way. However, we were still nervous enough not to make any stops.

The highway wound through hills and farmland. We were getting into the heart of the Ozarks. We passed

Doolittle and began to see signs for Vernelle's Motel.

"John's should be just past that motel," Kurt said.

The motel included a new-looking Cities Service gas station with a green-and-white motif and a shamrock-y looking sign.

A row of several rustic log cabins and a few newer white-sided units appeared further down the road. A neon sign boasted 'John's Modern Cabins'—a name that was somewhat belied by the outhouse that could be seen behind the office.

Kurt pulled the trailer into the parking lot and stopped. He pulled out his billfold and peered into it.

"I have ten dollars left. I'll offer a couple to the owner and see if he'll let us park right here. In case we don't make the switch tonight, we'll still have some for gas to get back to Times Beach. It looks like in that guide book that this area is still open in the twenty-first century. Can you guys wait here?"

"Sure," I said. "I think it's better anyway if we play the submissive little women."

He grinned. "Are you that good an actress?"

"Hush."

The sun was setting, creating long spooky shadows from the trees. The guide book showed photos of the cabins in our time as a few ruined derelicts—even spookier.

"I can't wait for this to be over," Dinah said from the back seat. I didn't comment. I just hoped it *would* be over.

While we waited, a rusty pickup pulled up, the driver got out, went into the office/snack bar and soon reappeared with a six pack of bottled beer.

Kurt returned and opened the door. "We're good. We can stay right where we are. He does have candy bars in there and ice cream bars."

"Awesome!" Dinah said.

We collected our personal items and moved back into the camper. Mother and I concocted an ersatz supper of a few slices of lunch meat, some iffy bread, and two small bags of potato chips. Dinah offered to get ice cream bars from the snack bar for dessert. We assigned her that heavy responsibility.

We crowded around our little table with the meager offerings, and the tension over the possible success of our evening's 'trip' was thick enough to spread on the sandwiches.

CHAPTER THIRTEEN
Linda

WE FINISHED OUR MODEST supper and Dinah suggested a game of cards. I was tired — mentally exhausted — and would have been happy to lay down with my book, but no one can turn down that pleading granddaughter look.

"Sure thing, dear. I wish I had a tall glass of ice water." I turned to my son-in-law. "Kurt, do they sell ice in that shop?"

"I don't think anyone sells bags of ice yet like we're used to, but I'm sure they'd put ice in a cup. There's a small bar at one end of the office. I'll check."

I waved him off. "I need the fresh air. I'll get it." I took a turquoise aluminum tumbler out of the cabinet and pulled on my cardigan.

"Don't go getting picked up by some sleaze, Linda." Kurt winked at me.

"Right." I let myself out the door.

The night had a little chill, and I pulled my sweater closer around me. It was a pleasant evening. Laughter and music spilled through the screen door of the small office and store. If it wasn't the wrong time and place, it would be great. I pushed the door open and glanced around. A group of four or five men sat around a small square table at one end of the room playing cards. Several beer bottles teetered on the corners of the table.

I went to the counter and spoke to a grizzled-looking man—John, perhaps?—counting money in the cash register drawer. He closed it quickly as I came close. I never thought I looked like a robber, but maybe so.

"Could I buy some ice?" I held out the tumbler.

He looked from the empty glass to me. "Ice?"

He seemed puzzled by the term, and I thought perhaps we had ended up in another country.

"I just want some ice water and need some ice cubes."

The request seemed to dawn rather slowly, but a warm smile spread across his face. His smile changed his visage from threatening to welcoming. "Oh, I see. Of course. Sorry—I was thinking about something else." He reached for the glass and took it back into a small kitchen. A plain looking woman of indeterminate age worked at the counter. Someone out of sight coughed almost continuously.

I watched John get trays out of a small freezer and take them to the sink to open them. I rubbed the side of my thumb, thinking of the numerous times I had pinched it on one of those tray handles.

A shout from the table startled me.

"Verl! You old dog! You hiding cards up your sleeve?"

I looked at the group. A blonde man facing me looked up and grinned, and a chill gripped my spine. Verl. It couldn't be. He looked at me with recognition too. "Lynette?" he called out.

I turned back just as John came back with my tumbler.

"Here you go. No charge."

I mumbled my thanks and rushed for the door. A hand grabbed my arm.

"Lynette?" he said again.

"You must have me mistaken for someone else," I said, turning my face toward him. His surprise told me that he realized then that I was much older than the woman he sought: my mother.

"Oh, excuse me, ma'am. I didn't mean—well, she doesn't even live around here, so not likely I'd run into her here, is it?"

"Probably not." I hurried out the door.

Outside, I collapsed on a bench beside the door and gasped for breath. I should have thought—a fishing camp like this—I knew he and his friends took lots of fishing trips in Missouri, even in later years when I knew him.

I wished I had somewhere I could go and be alone for

a bit until my heart stopped racing. I found a tissue in my pocket and mopped my forehead. The cool breeze felt good on my warm cheeks.

A blonde head poked out of the door. "Ma'am? Are you okay?"

"Yes, yes. I'm fine." I sprang up from the seat and hurried away. I walked in the opposite direction from the camper, but knew I had to get back soon. Lynne would wonder what had happened to me.

Thinking of my daughter reminded me of her concerns about this trip, or any time travel. She said the smallest changes could have wide-reaching effects and that there were many opportunities to 'screw up the world.' She had found that even changes with good intentions could have dire consequences.

I wrapped my arms around myself—protection, I guess—and forced myself to think about Verl. He rented a small, lean-to bedroom in the back of our house. My mother, Lynette, had an affair with him. If she was seeing him before I was born, it must have gone on for over ten years. Mother had a crazy, wild streak, as Dinah had found out on her own time travels.

I stumbled in a pothole and just caught myself before going down. I needed to get back. I had walked farther than I realized. I hurried back past the office. The laughter coming out of the door seemed more sinister to me now. What was I going to do?

When I reached the trailer, Lynne was coming down

the steps. "Oh, Mom! I was just coming to see what happened to you. Did you find ice?"

I held out the tumbler. "I did." Although it was starting to melt.

Lynne scrutinized my face. "What's wrong?"

"Nothing." I held back tears.

She took my arm and guided me away from the camper.

"Something is. Something's happened."

I shook my head. I needed to forget about the encounter, put it behind me. Otherwise I would do something *really* stupid.

"Mother. I'm *not* an idiot. In the last four days, you've time-traveled, been kidnapped, witnessed a shooting, and seen your son-in-law arrested. But you took it all in stride and when you left the camper to get ice, you were fine—or at least upbeat. Something happened."

I shrugged. "Maybe it's delayed shock."

She shook her head. "It could be, but I don't think that's it."

I took a deep breath. "There's a man in there." I couldn't go on.

She cocked her head. "Yes? Did he threaten you or something?"

"No. It's just that—I know him."

Her eyes widened. "Know him? How?"

"From home. He. . ." I stopped.

She waited, and when I didn't continue, said, "Mom.

Whatever it is, I think you need to talk about it. You look like you're ready to crumble."

After a moment and a couple of deep breaths, I said, "He had an affair with my mother. He called me by her name. After a closer look, of course, he realized his mistake." I tried to smile.

Lynne turned and stared off into the trees. "Wow. You said once she was pretty wild. What's he doing down here?"

"He is a big fisherman. He and his buddies come down here a lot, I think."

"So...you know this is all in the past, right?"

"Is it? I mean, I'm thinking I should do something to keep it all from happening."

Lynne looked sympathetic, almost pitying. "The affair, you mean?"

Now I looked off into the trees. A new moon slipped between the branches and wispy clouds sailed by. "I think that's already started. At least, they obviously know each other. No, it gets worse. I can't talk about that."

She hooked her arm in mine, giving me a little squeeze. "Let me know when you are ready to. But you know *my* experience. Sometimes when you try and change things—trying to avoid something bad, I mean— worse things happen." She guided me toward the camper. "Let's go in. Dinah's anxious to take you in rummy. Anyway, I don't know what you could do to end

123

this affair. Not unless you put out a contract on him."

She gave me another silly grin, but I blanched and jerked away from her. "Why would you say that?"

She put her hands up. "Just a joke, Mom!" Her voice dropped to a whisper. "Wait—is that what you're thinking? Do away with him?"

I scoffed. "Of course not—don't be silly. I know there's really nothing I can do."

She wasn't completely sold, but shook her head and continued toward the camper.

"WHAT TOOK SO LONG?" Dinah asked. "Are you trying to pick up guys again, Grandma?"

"Sorry. Just got to visiting with the owner. Ready for cards?"

I scooted into the dinette seat and noticed Kurt scrutinizing me. I couldn't keep my mind on the game and Dinah beat me three games in a row.

Lynne said, "Dinah, I think Grandma's really tired. It's been a rough couple of days."

Dinah gave me that adorable, impish grin of hers and said, "What, Grandma? A little kidnapping wears you out?"

I gave her hair a tweak and sighed. "I know. There was a time when I could get kidnapped three or four times in one day and think nothing of it."

Dinah laughed, but I caught a concerned look between Lynne and Kurt.

My head felt like it was in a vice; I definitely needed to talk some of this out. "Let's go out for another walk," I said to Lynne. "Then maybe I'll be able to sleep."

"Can I go?" Dinah asked.

"Why don't you set up the beds first?" Lynne said. "Then join us."

Dinah grumbled, and we slipped out the door. I heard Kurt trying to distract her. He realized, too, that there was a problem.

Lynne gripped my hand. "You're holding something back. I realize the affair would be upsetting, but it's in the past. It's over."

I looked up at the sky a minute.

"What happened to him?" Lynne asked.

"I don't know for sure."

"Did the affair end?"

"Oh, yes," I said.

"How old were you — do you remember?"

"Ten and a half."

She looked surprised. "You seem very sure — very exact."

"Yes. I am."

"Why?"

I shook my head and put my face in my hands. I wanted to put this burden down, but I didn't want to lay it on my daughter. The camper door slammed as Dinah came down the steps.

"Ready or not, here I come!" she trilled. "Is this hide and seek?"

Suddenly I wanted to be free of this conversation. "C'mon," I said, and grabbed Lynne's hand, pulling her into the trees along the parking lot. We ducked behind a sizable old oak.

We could hear Dinah shuffling around the gravel.

"Mom? This isn't funny."

Which of course made Lynne and I both giggle.

"Grandma? Where are you guys?"

She was getting closer.

Lynne moaned with a few haunting "Ooooooohs" thrown in for good measure.

Dinah said, "You guys don't scare me," but the bravado was a little obvious.

"YAWWK!" Lynne screeched as she jumped from behind the tree. Dinah fell back and screamed, and we all broke up in laughter.

I finally caught my breath. Such silliness was cathartic for my doldrums.

"Maybe we should go in and get ready for bed," I suggested.

"I thought we were going for a walk," Dinah said. "It's the least you could do after getting me all stirred up."

"You are such a con man," her mother said.

"Con girl. I mean, con woman!"

"All right—a short walk toward the road and back." I didn't want to pass the office again.

We linked arms and ambled along the rough gravel.

"I think this will be my last time travel trip," Dinah said. "There's just too many things that can go wrong."

I agreed. "First and last for me."

"I tried—" Lynne started, but I cut her off.

"I know. I know. You told us that. You were right."

"Hopefully, it will all be over soon," Dinah said. "No bracelets tonight."

"No bracelets tonight," Lynne agreed.

We continued our stroll, seeking peace in the quiet rural evening. The laughter from the office was a distant and now comforting backdrop.

An interruption to the peace came in the form of a '48 Plymouth screeching to a halt in front of the office. A teenaged boy jumped out of the passenger side and rushed inside. He was soon back with a brown paper sack bundled under his arm and the car took off.

Dinah frowned. "What's that about?"

"Your dad said John is known for selling beer to anyone—no questions asked. He also sells it on Sunday —that's illegal in Missouri—so he's known as 'Sunday John.'" Lynne said.

"How does Dad know that?" Dinah asked.

"His guide books." We had seen enough of those.

We stared up at the stars, more visible without the pervasive ambient light of our own times. Finally we turned back, as if of one mind, and headed to our beds.

But once tucked in, in the dark of the trailer, my ghosts came back to haunt me.

CHAPTER FOURTEEN

Lynne

MOTHER'S REVELATION WAS DISTURBING, and whatever she was holding back was even more concerning. I knew that my grandmother Lynette was a wild one. I'd heard stories, and then two years earlier, Dinah had time traveled to 1937 and spent some time with her great-grandmother as a fellow 14-year-old. Lynette was a free spirit who took nothing seriously. Her antics nearly got them both in deep trouble.

But the Lynette I knew as my grandmother was a totally different person. She died when I was seven or eight, but I remembered her as a crabby, sour old woman with a grudge against the world. The few photographs of her reflected the same unhappy countenance.

I lay there in the dark, hoping everything worked and in the morning we would be back in the twenty-first century. I swore to myself that I would never risk time travel again, nor would I allow my family to.

I must have dozed off, but the noise of a door closing gradually seeped into my subconscious. I had to reorient myself—where I was, what was at stake. And that it was the middle of the night. More minutes passed before I was awake enough to register what I had heard.

There were no sounds in the camper other than the soft breathing of sleep coming from Kurt beside me and someone in the other bed. Mother? Or Dinah? I didn't think anyone had come in and realized someone must have gone out.

I panicked. This could not be good. We couldn't make the time change and leave anyone behind. I threw the blanket back and rushed over to the other bed. With faint light coming through the window, I could just make out a single form. The long tangled hair told me that Dinah was there, but Mother was gone.

I nudged Dinah awake. "Dinah! Get up! We have to get out of here now. Kurt!" I dashed back to the couch bed and shook him. I didn't know when during the night the time change occurred or if it was always the same time. I didn't even know if we had to be asleep. All I knew was that we couldn't take a chance on leaving my mother in another century.

I badgered Kurt and Dinah to get them outside and into the Jeep. Dinah, with the resilience of youth, immediately curled up in her blanket in the back seat and went back to sleep. Kurt sat in the driver's seat, staring blankly out the windshield into the dark night.

"Where would she go?" he asked, shaking his head. *"Why* would she go?"

"I don't know." I explained what I knew from Mother's earlier revelation. "But something else is bothering her that she hasn't told me. She seemed to think she could stop the affair and whatever else happened, but I can't imagine how." Actually, I could imagine but I didn't want to think about that right now.

"Do you want me to help look for her?"

"No, I'd rather you stay with Dinah. I don't want to leave her alone here—seems to be a lot of single guys staying at this place. I'll look and check back with you. Wish our cell phones worked here."

"But then you're alone out there…"

"I have a can of pepper spray that I had in my purse." I held it up and then stuck it in my jacket pocket. I leaned over and gave him a kiss and a hug.

He closed the driver's door gently so as not wake Dinah and gave me a forlorn little wave. I knew he blamed himself for insisting on the time jump. For that matter, Mother also felt responsible. But all that mattered at this point was to get us all back safe and sound.

I took out a small flashlight that we kept in the Jeep and used it to avoid potholes and rocks in the road. I had no idea where Mother would go. Would she try and find this man that she knew? And if she found him, then what?

It was too awful to think about, but I couldn't come up with any other reason she would leave the trailer. She knew it was necessary to be in it to make the time jump. Something much deeper than what she had told me had to be behind her erratic behavior.

A row of mismatched cabins stretched along the road. Apparently the original cabins were the ones built out of logs, while later additions had white siding. The office was dark and the whole area quiet. A dog barked in the distance. Closer by, I could hear rustling in the trees — small animals, I hoped. The surrounding hills were barely silhouetted against the night sky.

I reached the end of the cabins, passing only a couple with lights still on. Could she have found this guy? But how? The office was closed and it didn't sound like she had talked to him long enough to find out where he was staying.

I went around behind the cabins, picking my way among scattered logs and branches. I passed the out house and jumped when the door creaked open and a young man stepped out. He nodded, put a finger to his forehead in a kind of salute, and walked around one of the cabins to the front.

I continued on my way and was about to give up and search the other direction from the camper, when a shape sitting on a log off in the trees moved, and I heard my name whispered.

"Mom? What are you doing out here?" I walked over

to her and sat beside her on the log. Her shoulders shook and I realized she was silently sobbing. I put my arm around her shoulders. "What is it? You obviously need to talk about this."

She held her hands between her knees and slowly pulled the right one out. The glow from the neon sign caught a reflection, and I turned my flashlight on what she held in her hand. It was a carving knife from the camper.

"*What* are you doing?" I gently removed the knife from her hand, but I could barely talk because I was sure what she had in mind.

"I don't know," she whispered.

"Who is this guy, and what did he do? I need some answers." Time for a little guilt, I thought. "You are endangering all of us by being out here. We probably won't be able to make the time change now."

She put her hands over her face. "Oh, Lynne. I'm so sorry. Verl—Verl James, that's his name—rented a room from us for years and, as I told you, had an affair with my mother."

"I know, and I realize that's upsetting, but unfortunately lots of people have affairs. It's not the end of the world."

"But that's not all. When I was about ten and a half, I came home from school one day, and he was the only one in the house. He—he attacked me. I was really scared, Lynne. I screamed, but no one came. Not right away.

Then I heard my mom come home. She started yelling and he left."

"What happened to him?"

She shrugged. There was a long pause before she said, "I don't know. He never came back for his stuff. My dad gave it to the Salvation Army."

She was still holding something back. "What do you *think* happened to him?"

"I think they killed him. My mom or my dad – or both. No one ever heard from him again. His sister came looking for him. She had him listed as a missing person, and the police came. You see, all of this agony because this man lived. I *hate* him." She looked at the knife in my hand.

I hugged her. "But you know this isn't the answer." I felt like I was talking to Dinah when she was seven or eight.

"He's going to die young anyway."

"You don't know that for sure. We need to let Kurt and Dinah know that I've found you."

I pulled her to her feet and we returned to the Jeep.

As we walked, she said, "Is it too late for the time change tonight?" The hopelessness in her voice chilled me. Where was my mother, the positive, confident optimist?

"I don't know – possibly."

"What am I going to do, Lynne?"

"Well, if we're stuck here another day, we can talk

about it. Maybe there is some way we can discourage this Verl from going back to your parents' house—I don't know what. What does he do? I mean, what was his job?"

"He worked for the railroad—he was a dispatcher."

"Let me think about this." We reached the Jeep. Kurt jumped out when he saw us.

"Linda! Are you okay? You had us worried."

Mother hung her head, still in the seven-year-old mode, and apologized.

Kurt hugged her. "Don't worry about it." He looked at me. "What are we going to do now?"

"It may be too late, but I say we go back to bed and see if we can still make the change tonight."

Mother's head snapped back up, and she looked as if I had betrayed her. "But you said…"

"I said *if* we were stuck here another day. But we are going to take every opportunity to get back to where we belong—above all else." I sympathized with Mother and what she had experienced, but the stakes were too high to not take even the slight chance that we could get back tonight.

Kurt looked from one to the other of us, and decided that I was being the parent here. He roused Dinah from the back seat and herded her back into the camper. Mother and I followed. I locked the door behind us. If she tried to go back out, it would make more noise and I could stop her.

I wanted badly to talk it all over with Kurt, but the camper didn't allow for private conversation. I just squeezed his hand when I got into bed beside him and whispered, "We'll talk in the morning."

I could tell he was puzzled by my behavior, and his loyalties were torn. I had always teased Mom that she liked Kurt better than me and that the feeling was mutual. But I desperately hoped in this instance that his greatest loyalty lay with me.

There was a lot of tossing and turning before we gradually dropped off.

CHAPTER FIFTEEN
Linda

THE SUN WAS PEEKING through the gap in the curtains, giving the interior of the camper a pleasant glow, even through my eyelids. It didn't help my mental or physical well-being. It was a cool morning. Dinah's warmth next to me was welcome, but the hangover I suffered from wouldn't be remedied by aspirin and coffee.

I refused to open my eyes. If I looked outside and saw only tumble-down cabins, it was too late to do anything. I could bury it in the nether regions of my brain again. If not, I still had an opportunity. But to do what?

I had been fascinated with Verl James when I was a kid. He was handsome and funny; he teased me and played games with me. When I got old enough to notice boys, my friends all fell in love with him. I trusted him and felt safe with him. Until that fateful Friday. And what happened after that? I didn't know. It was several years before it occurred to me that my parents might have had something to do with his disappearance. The more I thought about it, the more convinced I became.

I asked my dad when we cleaned out Verl's room. "Dad? Where did Verl go?"

He gave me a stern look. "No idea, but good riddance to bad rubbish as far as I'm concerned." I understood that the subject was closed.

I HEARD SOMEONE rustling around at the other end of the camper. And a groan. Lynne. We must still be in 1952. My stomach clenched. Now what?

I opened my eyes. "Lynne? What is it?" Of course, I knew.

"No change last night."

I sat up. "I'm sorry. I really am. I don't know what I was thinking."

She sighed. "I know, Mom. But, you know, I tried to warn you of the potential for disaster." She was tired and disgusted with me. I couldn't blame her.

I got up and grabbed my clothes—a wrinkled mess of non-permanent press. I found my jeans instead.

"Get dressed," she said, "and let's go outside and talk. Let them sleep."

Outside, we stood and watched the cabins stir to life —fisherman leaving (no sign of Verl) and a few who appeared to be headed to jobs. There was nowhere to sit. We hadn't brought lawn chairs because we didn't plan to be sitting around. We hadn't planned on much of anything that had happened.

"I think there's a restaurant at that Vernelle's Motel that we passed. We could walk back there. Maybe we could all do with a big breakfast." I tried to suggest something upbeat.

"We don't have enough money—not the right kind. We need to hoard every cent until we get back," Lynne said.

She wouldn't look at me. She was the parent and I was the naughty child. I didn't remind her that none of the last two days would have happened if she hadn't forgotten to take the bracelet off. But, that was an accident; I *knowingly* left the camper and caused the delay the previous night.

We had both opted for jeans and white blouses. Our other clothes were beyond salvage. Lynne had pulled her hair back into a pony tail tied up with a bright pink scarf. She looked very cute, but I knew she didn't care at this point.

"Let's walk over to the office and see if there's a couple of cheap snacks we can afford."

Ouch.

We had enough change for a box of Ritz crackers and a package of Lifesavers. My stomach grumbled just thinking about what a long day it was going to be. When we came out, I noticed Verl and one of the card players hitching a john boat to a pickup. He looked up, and other than curiosity, showed no emotion.

Lynne noticed me staring. "Is that him?"

"Yes."

"Let's walk that way."

"Lynne, I don't want to talk to him." I pulled back.

"We're not going to talk to him. I just want to get a better look."

I tried to hide behind her, but Verl was busy at his task and didn't pay us any further attention. Lynne put her hand firmly behind my back to keep me moving forward. As we got farther down the road, I whispered "Why did you want to know last night what his job was?"

"Just a wild idea that maybe we could find him a job down here in his favorite fishing territory. But I forget that we don't have the internet yet, barely any gas, cell phones don't work. I don't think we could do it. There's something familiar about him. Have I seen pictures of him?"

"No, I burned the few I found in my mother's things after she died. I just wish I could keep him from going back there. If my mother had anything to do with his disappearance, it would explain the change in her personality. She hardly ever laughed after that."

Lynne was quiet for several minutes as we looped around to the road and back toward the camper.

"I can't think of anything we can do to keep him away from Grandma," she said finally.

"There is one thing," I said.

"I can't believe you would even think that." Her voice cracked. "It must have been a terrible experience for you."

"I grew up fast after that."

"But besides the obvious objections to...removing him permanently, you don't know what else you would change."

I sighed. "I would have had a happier childhood. And a happier mother."

"Well," Lynne said, "I hate playing the parent here, but since I have more experience, I can definitely tell you that time travel is a 'be careful what you wish for' kind of thing. You don't know that would be true."

The pickup pulling the boat passed us and turned out on to the gravel road, stirring up a cloud of dust. We turned around and headed back to the camper.

Lynne grabbed my arm. Her face was pale and her eyes were wide. "Mom, I just figured out why he looks familiar. He looks a lot like you."

"What?!"

"Maybe it's my imagination, but, what if..." She couldn't finish, couldn't say it.

"He's my biological father?" I whispered.

She nodded, tears welling up in her eyes. "This is what I mean about changing the past. There are so many unknowns—we can't take the chance."

CHAPTER SIXTEEN
Dinah

THE SUN WAS UP and the camper was light. I grabbed my pillow and buried my face in it. If nobody woke me up, that was not a good sign. We hadn't made the time change. What was wrong with my grandma that she would go out in the middle of the night like that? She had always been smart and cool. They weren't telling me something.

Every day that we were stuck in 1952 made me think more and more that we would never get back. I would never see my friends again. I would never know whether Brad Bronsky would ask me out. I certainly wouldn't go to college to be a computer programmer. And what would happen when we reached the year we were supposed to be born? Would Grandma Linda turn into a baby the next year? And my parents in twenty or so more years? And me after that?

For once I agreed with my mom. There was just too much crap we didn't know to be messing around with this time travel stuff. But it made me mad that they left me out of all the decisions. No one cared what I thought.

I opened my eyes, rolled over, and threw back the blanket. No one else was here. I had a another scary thought. What if they *had* made the time change and I hadn't?

I was shaking a little bit as I pulled on my jeans and slipped my feet into loafers. Then I heard talking outside and felt a huge relief when I recognized my dad's voice. They were all outside. I joined them.

"What's going on?"

My mom smiled at me—but not a happy smile—and said, "We didn't make the change last night. We'll have to try again tonight." Like she would say "We forgot to get pork chops so we're having meat loaf. Ho-hum." I was beginning to wonder if they really *wanted* to make the change.

I knew they wouldn't listen to me, so I said, "I'm hungry. Do we have anything to eat?"

Grandma Linda held up a familiar red box. "We got some Ritz—and Lifesavers." She handed me the roll of candies.

"Huh!" I said. "That's a dumb name. Like those'll keep us from starving to death."

I saw Daddy give my mom 'a look.' You know, the 'she's being difficult' look. What do they expect when they take a kid away from their home and friends and into a different century? And are out of food besides?

Daddy pulled a little change out of his pocket. He counted out a few coins. "I noticed last night that they have Twinkies in the office. Do you want to go get yourself some?"

He was either feeling bad for me or they wanted to talk privately. I took the money. "Should I get them for every one?"

"There's just enough change there for one package," he said. That made me feel kind of guilty, but I was really hungry, so I went.

There was a lady at the counter in the office. Her hair was fixed in tight little curls and she was wearing a faded flowered dress. She looked tired. I got my Twinkies and waited behind an old guy to pay. A door behind her was open and coughing came from somewhere in the back. The lady kept looking over shoulder and she looked worried.

When it was my turn, I asked, "Is someone sick?"

"My little girl," she said. "She just has a sore throat. But she's kind of bored and wants a lot of attention."

She gave me a nickel in change and I put it in my pocket. I had a sudden idea that would help me fill the time on what looked like was going to be a long day. Besides, I couldn't imagine how boring it would be to be sick without TV, phones, or iPads.

"I could read to her," I said. "I don't have anything to do today."

She gave me a big smile. "Oh, would you? I'll be right here, but my husband is gone today and I have to take care of the office. That would be wonderful!"

"Sure. I'll go tell my parents."

WHEN I GOT BACK to the camper, Mom, Dad, and Grandma were inside sitting at the dinette, looking serious and munching on Ritz crackers.

"Um, the lady in the office has a little girl who isn't feeling well. I told her I would read to her since I don't have anything else to do." I guess that came out a little whiny, but it was the truth.

Grandma Linda said, "Oh, Dinah, that would be so nice of you."

Mom wasn't sure it was a good idea. "How sick is she? I don't want you to catch anything."

"She just has a cold," I said.

Mom and Dad both nodded.

"I'm going to have one of my Twinkies first and then I'll go back over there."

I realized that the little package might be my only food for the day. I only ate half of one and then carefully wrapped it back up.

"Here I go. You can go back to your plotting."

At least they looked a little guilty.

AT THE OFFICE, the woman at the counter — who introduced herself as Mrs. Bachmeier — put a little "Be Right Back!" sign on the counter and motioned me through the kitchen door in the back. The kitchen had a couch and chair at one end and two doors, one closed and one open.

I followed Mrs. Bachmeier through the open door. A little girl in the bed looked at me with kind of red eyes. I guess she was about seven or eight years old and was piled with blankets even though it was pretty warm outside. A folded, wet washcloth covered her forehead.

"Betty, honey, this is — ?" She looked at me.

"Dinah," I said.

"Dinah, and she said she would read to you for a little bit. Isn't that nice of her?"

Betty nodded and pointed at a stack of books on a table. "*Five Little Peppers*" she said in a quiet, hoarse voice.

"She loves those books," Mrs. Bachmeier said to me. She picked up the top one.

Betty shook her head. "No, I already read that one. *Five Little Peppers at School*." She was thin and pale and her hair was pretty stringy.

Mrs. Bachmeier searched through the stack and handed me a tattered green book. "Have you read them?"

"I don't think so."

"They're very old books. Her grandma gave them to

her." She turned to Betty, removed the washcloth, and felt the little girl's forehead. "Are you feeling any better, dear?"

"No."

Her mother shook her head. "We may have to call the doctor. We'll see how you are this afternoon. I'll get you a fresh glass of water. Dinah, there's a chair by the window you can bring over."

I carried the wooden chair to the bedside, sat down, and opened the book. Mrs. Bachmeier returned with the water glass. "I'll be right in the office if you need me. Thank you so much." And she was gone.

"How come you haven't read *Five Little Peppers*? Don't you read books?"

"Yes, I read a lot." I'd better not mention Harry Potter. "Um, I read a lot of Nancy Drew books." I knew those were old.

"My mom says I'll be old enough for those next year." She coughed and blew her nose.

"Well, we'd better get started, hadn't we?" I began reading. Some of the words were odd—words I knew, but they didn't seem to be used in the same way. Betty stopped me occasionally to ask a question or blow her nose again. I took several breaks when she had coughing or sneezing fits. My throat started to get dry and I glanced at the glass of water.

Betty saw me looking. "You can have some."

"I'd better not. I don't want to catch your cold. But thanks for the offer."

"Mom gets me a clean glass every time," Betty said.

"Okay, I'll just take a little sip." I did. "How long have you been sick?"

"About a week." She paused and twisted a strand of light brown hair around her finger. "You're really pretty."

"Oh! Thank you!"

"Are you in *high school?*" She sounded like she was in awe.

"I'm going to be in eleventh grade next year."

"Wow." She stared at the ceiling a minute and then turned her face back to me. "Can you read some more?"

"Sure." We continued on the story.

Mrs. Bachmeier appeared in the doorway a little later. "Would you girls like some lunch? I have some leftover meatloaf for sandwiches."

My stomach growled so loud, I was afraid she could hear it. Lunch! And I thought I was going to have to subsist on Twinkies.

"I would love some." I tried not to sound too eager.

"Can I have soup instead?" Betty asked.

Her mother bent over her, doing a forehead check again. "That's a good idea. I'll be back in a few minutes."

Betty whispered, "She has cookies out there, too."

"Yum. Which of the Five Little Peppers do you like best?"

"Polly," she stated. "But I do like Phronsie's name. Isn't that a neat name?"

"It is. I've never heard it before."

"And she has blonde curly hair. I wish I did."

We talked about the good and bad points of curly hair until her mother came back with a tray and her soup. She propped Betty up in the bed and the tray had little legs so it wouldn't tip. Betty crumbled up a handful of crackers, took a couple of bites, and then just stirred the soup.

When her mother came back with my sandwich, Betty handed off the tray. "I guess I'm not very hungry." Mrs. Bachmeier helped her lay back down.

Betty yelped. "Ow!"

"What's the matter?"

"My head hurts when I move."

"*Where* does your head hurt?" Mrs. B. was starting to sound a little tired of Betty's symptoms.

Betty put a hand on the back of her neck. "Here."

Mrs. B. straightened up and looked scared.

"I'll take your temperature. When did this headache start?"

"This morning." She sounded bad but she might have been acting. Sometimes I baby sit with a neighbor girl. She pretends she sick all the time, but she's pretty fakey. Betty's cheeks were really red.

Mrs. Bachmeier stood up and shook the thermometer. "I'm going to call Dr. Stanley. Your fever is really high." Betty sneezed and just looked at us with watery eyes.

I took my plate out to the kitchen sink. Mrs. Bachmeier followed me and I thanked her for the sandwich. "Do you want me to help Betty get dressed?" I asked.

"For what?"

"To go to the doctor's office?"

She shook her head. "Oh, no. He'll come here. Taking her out would just make her worse."

Then I remembered hearing about doctors making 'house calls' in the old days. That must be what she meant.

"What do you think she has?"

She let out a big sigh. "It probably is just a cold. But with the stiff neck — well, I'm sure your mother worries about the same thing. We've had several cases of polio around here already this summer. I don't want to take any chances." She smiled at me as she picked up the phone. "I really thank you for spending time with her this morning, but you probably better leave.

She turned and spoke into the phone. "Yes, this is Angela Bachmeier. It's about Betty."

I went back into the bedroom to find that Betty had dozed off. I put the chair and the book back and returned to the kitchen.

"Thanks again for lunch," I said as I left. "I hope she's better soon." I let myself out and walked back to the camper. I had heard about polio but didn't know any one in my time who had it. The motel court was very quiet, and flies buzzed around a garbage can.

CHAPTER SEVENTEEN

Lynne

I WAS RELIEVED that Dinah had found something to occupy her time on this long day. We were so restricted. Our little money and gas were about gone, and we didn't dare stray far from the camper for fear it might disappear again.

Mother's mental state bothered me more than anything. She was very depressed after spotting Verl James. I couldn't wrap my head around the concept of my mom harming—well, eliminating—anyone, no matter the circumstances. Yet she seemed perfectly willing to do that, until I pointed out her resemblance to the man. Since then it was worse than shock. She barely functioned.

I was glad that Dinah was not around to see her beloved grandmother disintegrate. They had always been close. Dinah was the only grandchild and Kurt's parents were gone. Mother tolerated Dinah's most outrageous behavior — behaviors that she never would have stood for when I was a child. She good-naturedly ignored our suggestions for restraint. I had long since decided that this total acceptance was the function of grandparents.

After Dinah left, we sat at the dinette and discussed our situation. We concluded we had very few options, considering our lack of resources. I asked Mother to tell Kurt about her experience with Verl. He sat speechless as she told her story.

At the end, he took her hand and said, "I'm sorry, Linda."

Her smile was weak, but there nonetheless. "Not your fault."

"I know, but I'm still sorry it happened to you."

She put her head in her hands. "I know I need to move on. It's past." She looked up. "But then again, it isn't, you know?"

"I know. That's the problem. But you've put this behind you before. Do you think you can again?"

"I don't know. It's like I've been holding my breath my whole life, and now I can't get my breath." She stared out the window.

Her depression disturbed me. This wasn't going to be something that she would 'snap out of.'

What would she have done in my place if I was crushed, paralyzed by some event in my life? When I was much younger, she would have distracted me. Dinah had the right idea. At Mother's age, I wasn't sure what she would do, so I would go with distraction.

"I know we can't buy anything, but maybe we should check out Vernelle's. I noticed other buildings there near the restaurant. Give us something to do."

"Sure," Mother said, with little interest.

We left Kurt to guard the camper and walked down the road away from John's. A flashy new neon sign was being wired in front of the motel and restaurant. Construction appeared to be ongoing on both the restaurant and another building. A sign leaned sideways against the second structure that said 'Gifts'. In spite of the unfinished look, a hand-lettered sign in the window said 'Open.'

"Let's go in," I said. Mother followed like an obedient puppy.

The place smelled new, even if the half-empty shelves didn't give it away. A trim woman in slacks and a blouse glanced up at us from a box she was unpacking. Her hair was tied back under a scarf, but her makeup looked fresh.

"Good morning!" she chirped. "Can I help you with something?"

"We're just browsing," I said. "It looks like you've just opened."

"Last week." She wiped her hands on her slacks as she stood up. "In fact, the outside isn't done yet, but I couldn't wait."

"Are you the owner?" I asked.

She stood and held out her hand. "Yes, I'm Vernelle. My husband and I bought the motel from his uncle recently and we added the restaurant and gift shop, and last month the Cities Service gas station."

"Wow! That's ambitious."

Mother wandered up and down the aisles, ignoring us.

The woman nodded. "It's keeping us busy. But it's a great location, you know, on 66. Are you just traveling through?"

"Um, yes. We're pulling a travel trailer and staying in that, but we—ah—had car trouble and can't move on until tomorrow. We thought we would walk up here and see what was going on."

Vernelle proceeded to pull china figurines of animals out of the box, wipe each off with a cloth, and arrange them on an empty shelf. "That's too bad about the car trouble. Who's fixing it for you?"

Ooops. I waved my hand. "Oh, I don't remember. My husband took care of it. Someone local, I guess."

I heard Mother moan and looked with alarm toward the aisle in the back of the store where she had disappeared. Now what? I hurried in that direction.

She stood clutching a doll. Platinum blonde wavy hair cascaded over her arm. She fingered the bright red outfit and glanced up at me.

153

"I had one of these when I was little—a Mary Hartline doll. I loved the Super Circus show and was heartbroken when it was cancelled."

Vernelle had followed me and looked at Mother perplexed. "But that doll just came out this year. You couldn't have had one when you were a girl. It must have been something similar." She spoke to Mother as if she was a small, confused child.

We needed to move on. It seemed evident that Vernelle would chalk Mother's statements up to senility, but there was no sense in dragging this out.

"Come on, Mom. Let's put it back and go see if Kurt got the car fixed."

"What happened to the car?" She didn't look disoriented or senile at all—just a mature, capable woman carrying on a casual conversation.

Vernelle was still standing behind me, so I winked at Mom as I patted her hand. "You remember, it made that noise, and he had to find someone to work on it." I am nothing if not a technical expert. The expression on her face told me that she finally realized what she had said about the doll.

"Oh, okay."

"Thank you for letting us look around." I took the doll from Mother and handed it to Vernelle.

She watched us go, the doll still in her arms. "Nice to meet you," she said, rather tentatively, and went to return the doll to the shelf.

Once outside, we headed back down the road to John's Modern Cabins.

"I'm really sorry, Lynne. I wasn't thinking. I don't know what's wrong with me."

"You've had a shock—a big one. The sooner we get back to our own time, the better."

She didn't answer and just kept her eyes on the road below her feet.

Kurt glanced up from his Route 66 guidebook as we walked in.

"Find anything interesting?"

I told him about Vernelle's and my story about the car. "Let's hope she doesn't come or send someone down here to 'help us out.' I don't think she will but you never know."

"Why did you even tell her that story?"

I plopped down on the couch. "You know me—I always feel I have to explain everything, whether someone asks me or not. I guess I thought she might ask why we were in the area, why we didn't stay at their motel or something. I don't know. What are you looking at?"

Kurt brushed his hair off his forehead. "Well, assuming that we get out of here tomorrow morning—in our own time, I mean—there's some interesting sites in the next county. Some old cabins, a spring that was on the Trail of Tears. Waynesville looks like a great lunch stop."

He noticed Mother hadn't said anything. "How are you doing, Linda?"

"I'll be fine," she said, with no evidence that that would happen.

Dinah came in. She looked a little sad.

"How did your morning go?" I asked.

"Fine. Betty's a sweet kid. But I think she's feeling worse and the doctor's coming this afternoon. She's asleep now."

"Oh dear," Mother said. "What's wrong with her?"

"She has a sore throat and she's running a fever. She didn't eat much for lunch." Dinah had a guilty little smile. "They gave me a meat loaf sandwich and cookies."

I groaned. "That sounds good. It's amazing how hungry we get just because we don't have food at our fingertips. I know we aren't going to starve to death, but a meatloaf sandwich right now sounds like a steak dinner."

Dinah sat on the couch. "Betty's mother called the doctor because she's worried about polio." She looked at us with a puzzled expression. "I don't know much about it."

"Oh dear. We've all been vaccinated but the vaccine wasn't available until 1955." I told them about the conversation I'd overheard at breakfast a couple of days before. "It was a huge worry for everyone."

THE DAY DRAGGED more than even the previous days.

We walked around the frontage road, played cards, and read. I was careful not to let Mother go out alone. I hoped she was accepting the situation, but I couldn't be sure.

Dinah had fallen asleep curled up at one end of the couch, so I went out to sit in the sun for a bit. It was a pretty day. The trees paraded their early summer canopy and dragonflies went about their busy-ness. Kurt joined me.

"I'm worried about your mother."

"Me, too. I will be so glad when we get away from this place, and we don't have to worry about running into that creep."

Kurt shrugged. "You're right. You know, there's no reason we can't move on now and try and make the time change somewhere else. She has a better chance of putting that experience behind her again the sooner she doesn't have to look at that guy."

I hadn't considered that possibility, but it made sense.

He went on. "I know we didn't want to get too far from Times Beach, in case we had to go back. But another twenty or thirty miles isn't going to make that much difference"

"What about gas?" I said.

"If we need to, we'll risk putting leaded gas in it. Better we have to buy a new car, if it comes to that, than not be able to get back to our own time. What do you think?"

"It's a great idea. We all need to move on, but especially Mom." I squeezed his hand. "Thanks for being so thoughtful of her."

"I have my moments. Let's get things put away. While we do, I'll tell you what's available in the next county."

CHAPTER EIGHTEEN

Lynne

I KNEW KURT WORRIED about Mother's state of mind, but I could also tell that he was excited to explore more of Route 66 in 1952.

"It looks like Waynesville is about twenty miles. Lebanon is about forty beyond that, but there's a lot to see before Waynesville. The main thing is to find a parking spot that will still be there in 2016. I think Laughlin Park, where the Cherokee camped on the Trail of Tears, might be a farm now. One of my books says the farmer donates the land in 1971. The trouble will be finding it now."

Mother was folding clothes and bedding and putting it away. She had made no comment. I put my hand on her shoulder. "You understand why we're doing this, don't you? We're worried about you. Besides, we feel that we all need to move on."

"I know."

We finished in record time and went outside the camper. I watched Kurt put the rest of the gas from the can into the Jeep's tank. Dinah walked to the office for a report on Betty. Mrs. Bachmeier said the doctor was fairly confident that she did not have polio, but they were going to keep a sharp eye on her.

Everyone piled into the Jeep and Kurt pulled away from John's Modern Cabins. In the side mirror, I could see Verl James watching us go. He was just putting a small suitcase in his truck.

I GLANCED OVER at the gas gauge once we were on the road. "What do you think?" I asked Kurt.

"There was more in the can than I thought. It should get us to Waynesville easily and then, assuming we make the change tonight, we can fill up tomorrow." He grinned at me, but it was forced. I think we were all hesitant to "assume" the change would take place after so many screw ups.

I tried to put it out of my mind and concentrate on the scenery. The day had clouded over, but the hills were spectacular. The road was tree-lined, and we were, according to the ads, in the "heart of the Ozarks." A few miles down the road, Kurt pointed out a dead end road leading to the dying town of Arlington. A change in the route of 66 in the 1940s had already cut it off, long before I-44 would go in.

"There were big changes during the war because Fort Leonard Wood is just south of here and they needed to move men and materials more efficiently."

I tried to show interest, but both Mother and Dinah were silent in the back seat. I hoped Dinah was just bored and not starting to feel poorly. I was still concerned that she might have caught something from Betty.

Stone bluffs rose up on both sides of the road. Kurt continued his travelogue. "This is the Hooker Cut. Part of that straightening project during the war. At this time, it's supposed to be the deepest cut in the country."

Still no response from the back seat. I half turned. "Dinah, honey, are you feeling okay?"

"Yes, Mother." That's a sign of trouble—any time I'm 'Mother' instead of 'Mom.'

I raised one eyebrow at her.

"There's nothing to see." She gave a long-suffering sigh. Maybe just teenaged boredom.

Kurt started to respond and then just satisfied himself with a grimace. This was not the hill we were going to die on this trip. Figuratively speaking, of course.

As we were coming out of the cut, the sun broke through the clouds, producing a stunning sunset framed by the cut. Pinks, purples, and golds streaked the sky. Dinah hung over the seat to peer out the windshield.

"Oh, that's pretty," she said. I relaxed a little.

Kurt turned left along a side road. "We're just going

161

to take a little detour here—a couple of miles. This is the original 66 before the cut, and I want us to see the Devil's Elbow."

"Just so we don't run short of gas. And we need to find a place to park before dark." I couldn't let Kurt's research goals interfere with making our best attempt to get back.

He kept going, of course. "There's the Elbow Inn—still there in 2016." He slowed down as we approached the bridge. "I'm looking for Temporal Road—there." He swung to the left in a wide curve onto a gravel road. In a short distance we were overlooking a wide river—the Big Piney, he said.

"Do you want me to drive?" I asked.

He was craning his neck to see the river and the road didn't have much for shoulders. The river was along our right and bluffs hugged the road on the left.

"No, I'm fine. There's a spot up here where I hope we can pull off and see the 'elbow.'"

"What's the big deal?" Dinah said.

"I'll explain when we stop."

We reached a slightly wider spot in the road where the trees and brush along the river had been cut back. He eased to a stop and we got out. The river made a complete U around the town of Devil's Elbow. Kurt explained how years before 'rafters' floated railroad ties down the river in rafts, some as long as a mile. When they got to the Elbow, some of the rafts would not make the turn on the U and get hung up on a huge boulder that the rafters claimed only the devil could have put there.

Back in the car, I said "Does this road hook back up with 66?"

"No. We have to turn around. There's a railroad trestle bridge farther down this road that looks interesting. But we'll skip that; you're right. We need to move on."

However, we saw the trestle bridge, because we couldn't find anywhere to turn the Jeep and trailer around until we had passed the bridge. So actually we saw it twice.

Evening fast approached as we returned to 'old' 66, drove across the 1923 bridge into the town of Devil's Elbow, and headed a few miles back to 'new' 66. This was one of the stretches of cement highway with curbs along the sides. One of those safety ideas that caused more accidents than it prevented.

Four or five more miles brought us to St. Roberts — not much of a town, since it had only been founded the year before. Mother had been quiet the entire trip. I desperately hoped we would make the time change that night, and maybe she could begin to adjust.

Kurt peered into the area illuminated by our headlights. "We're coming in to Waynesville. We need to watch for the creek crossing — we'll turn left there and hopefully find an open spot."

"I'm hungry," Dinah said.

I pumped my fist up. "Good! You haven't lost your appetite."

She stuck her tongue out at me.

"I mean it. That's a good sign that you aren't getting sick."

"Poor Betty. What if she does really have polio?"

Mother finally spoke, surprising us all. "Most cases were the non-paralytic type and people recovered. The more serious ones were often treated in an iron lung."

I turned to look at Dinah. She seemed pale and her mouth hung open. "What? That sounds like some kind of medieval torture."

Mother patted her hand. "I'm sorry, dear. I didn't mean to frighten you. Really, there's a very good chance she will be fine."

"I hope so." She lapsed back into silence.

"There's a bridge. Is that the creek?" I pointed ahead.

"I think so." Kurt leaned forward over the steering wheel. "Just in time, too. Looks like fog moving in."

I hadn't noticed the halos appearing around the street lights and mist on the streets. We turned down a gravel road bordered by hills on one side and fields on the other.

"Roubidoux Springs should be on our right. As I said, it's been designated a park in our time. If there's open area near the spring, we should be able to park there without a problem. The fog might be a blessing — keep anyone from noticing us since this is private property."

The fog thickened fast. It should hide us well, because

I could barely see past the fence line. Kurt stopped at a break in the fence.

"This might be it. I'll have to scout it out. Can you get the flashlight out of the glove box?"

I rummaged around and found two. Amazingly enough, both worked. "I'll go with you."

To me, nothing is eerier than fog at night. You feel like you're walking around in syrup. At least, what I think syrup would feel like. I kept my light on the ground and followed Kurt. Long weeds and grass clutched at our feet and unidentified shapes hovered at the periphery of my vision. Trees, I hoped.

Kurt stopped so suddenly that I hit him in the back with my light. Ahead of him, his light reflected off water in a large round pool.

"This is the spring. There's plenty of room to park if we can get it in here without hitting anything."

"I'll drive," I said. "You figure out a path that won't get us stuck."

As we walked back toward our headlights, we picked up any large sticks that could cause a problem and threw them to the side. An area where the ditch had been filled in created a barely drivable entrance.

I got in the driver's side and instructed Mother and Dinah to watch out the side windows as well as they could for any hazards.

"Are you going to back in?" Dinah asked.

"Not in this soup," I said. "We'll hope for much better

visibility in the morning to turn it around or back out." *Hope* was becoming the most common word in my vocabulary. I hoped Mother would get better, Dinah would not get sick, the fog would disappear, and above all, we would wake up in 2016. This was an alien feeling for me.

Hope meant things were out of my control. I didn't like it.

As I edged forward, both the Jeep and the camper rocked from one pothole to another. We managed to get parked without ending up in the spring. I lit a couple of candles inside the camper to save on our waning battery power.

We dined on the rest of the crackers and Dinah, no doubt feeling a little guilty about that meatloaf sandwich, shared the rest of her package of Twinkies. Kurt had refilled the water jugs when we were at John's, and, while I would have enjoyed a glass of a nice red wine, at least we weren't going to dehydrate. And maybe I would lose a few pounds. While we toyed with our food to make it last longer, Kurt told us about the historical significance of this place.

"The Cherokee camped here on the Trail of Tears because of the springs. I think the town started shortly after that. Missouri militia were stationed here during the Civil War."

By the time we finished, it was justifiably bedtime.

I said, looking at each one, "Tonight's rules are: No

Fifties jewelry. No getting arrested. No leaving the camper. Agreed?"

"What if that doesn't work? We're not in the same place that we came back in time," Dinah said.

"I know. We don't know that *won't* work—we've just never tried it. We'll deal with that if it happens. Let's plan on the result we want." And I knocked on the camper's paneling. Fortunately there was an abundance of wood in the camper.

The fog muffled the area from outside noise. The subdued bubbling of the springs quickly put me to sleep.

CHAPTER NINETEEN

Lynne

I WOKE IN THE MIDDLE of the night. Soft breathing and muffled snores floated in the little trailer. I thought about the past several days and all of our ups and downs. Mostly downs. We did get a good look at life on the Mother Road in the early Fifties, but at what price?

Somehow, when this commitment was over, I needed to find a way to get rid of this trailer. As long as we had it, there would always be "good" reasons to use it — with bad results.

I think I dozed several times but then would return to a semi-conscious state, my mind tumbling through seemingly unrelated thoughts. A constant background was the low grumble of the spring.

At some point, the noise seemed slightly louder. Flash floods were a problem in the spring and early summer in this hilly country, but there hadn't been any rain in the last few days. I corrected myself. There hadn't been any rain in our last few days in the Fifties, but what if we had made the time change and heavy rain was a factor in 2016? The despair I felt was like a weight holding me down. I wanted to look outside, but I couldn't.

The quality of the sound changed. It was still a low rumble but now it almost sounded like voices. Nothing distinct, but like the crowd on a sports event on TV. Now and then, a shout or a moan separated itself from the undercurrent. I sat up and pulled back a curtain to peek out a side window.

It was pitch dark and yet the grayness of the fog was evident. Shapes materialized and faded again into the amorphous mass. The camper seemed surrounded by people — occasionally I spotted a Civil War forage cap or a blanket-wrapped figure topped by a turban. Chills ran through my body. I was in the throes of a nightmare brought on by Kurt's description of this place's history. I had conjured hundreds of ghosts to people the springs.

A louder crash drowned out the voices — thunder. The figures disappeared. Cracks and booms sounded, as drenching rain began. I lay back down and shook as I tried to wrap my head around what I thought I had seen. Kurt stirred in his sleep and encircled me with his arm to still my shaking. The warmth calmed me and put me in dreamless sleep.

CHAPTER TWENTY

Lynne

RAIN. RAIN SPATTERED on the roof of the trailer and rain dribbled down the windows when I tried to look outside. Since it had been so foggy the night before, I really couldn't tell if anything had changed. In the gray light, I could see the pool of the spring where our flashlights had caught it when we arrived, but I didn't know if the retaining wall surrounding one side had been there or not. I lay there trying to shake off the effects of my dream.

"Mom?" A quiet whisper from the other end of the camper. "Are we back?"

I went over to her and perched on the edge of the bed. She looked exhausted, firing up my worries about her health and exposure to Betty's illness, whatever it was. "I can't tell, since we couldn't see anything last night to compare it to."

Kurt sat up and peered out the window. He squinted at us. "What do you think?"

I repeated what I had told Dinah. "But it sounds like the rain is letting up. I say we get dressed and go out and check it out."

He nodded and began folding up our blankets.

"I'm really hungry," Dinah said, reaching for a pair of sweatpants.

"Me too. I'm starved."

Mother began stirring, turned toward us an opened one eye. "What's going on?"

Again with the uncertain report. "We're going to go out and check. Regardless of the time frame, we need to figure out the best way to get out of here."

She nodded and pulled the blanket over her head. Behavior I expected more from my daughter than my mother.

Kurt and I dressed and pulled our rain gear out of a cupboard. When we got outside, he looked toward the spring and the retaining wall.

"I'm pretty sure that I read that was added later because of flooding washing out the road."

I gripped his hand. "I hope so." I was feeling desperate.

Dinah joined us. "What's that sign?" She pointed at a tilted story board mounted on posts. We walked toward it and Kurt bent over it. He straightened up and grinned.

"It's part of the new Wayside Exhibit—just put in last year. That is, 2015."

Dinah hugged us both, tears running down her cheeks. "Can we find a McDonald's?"

"We'll find something—like an all-you-can-eat breakfast buffet," he promised.

She giggled and looked back at the story board. The smile disappeared and she pointed at one of the figures depicted on the board. "What is he wearing? On his head?"

Kurt looked and said, "A turban. Common headdress among the southeastern tribes."

"Why?" I asked her.

She shook her head. "Nothing." She wouldn't look at me. Something niggled at me about her question but I couldn't isolate it.

"Let's go give Grandma the good news and find a place to eat ourselves sick." I hooked my arm in hers and dragged her toward the camper. She perked up a little at the mention of food.

AN HOUR LATER we had returned to 66, gassed up the Jeep with unleaded gas, and were on the search for a good old comfort food restaurant. Dinah stayed upbeat and Mother seemed more relaxed. Kurt and I were giddy.

He spotted a low gray building with a sign that announced 'Kountry Bufay.' He carefully locked up the Jeep and the camper. "I hope they cook better than they spell."

We trooped inside.

I'm usually kind of picky about restaurants, but the smells that assaulted my senses as we walked in almost made me into a drooling fool. A waitress scooped up menus from the hostess station and led us past a long buffet table to a booth. She pulled out a tablet and a pencil.

"Want some time to look at the menu?"

Kurt said, "I think we all want the buffet." He looked at the rest of us. We wagged our heads like a bunch of puppies.

She stuck the pencil behind her ear. "Good choice. You can go to the buffet line when you're ready."

I hoped she got out of the way so we didn't run her over. Actually, we restrained ourselves pretty well and walked in an orderly fashion to the line. But we didn't waste any time either.

When we returned to the booth, Dinah grinned from ear to ear as she plopped down a plate heaped with waffles, eggs, bacon, sausage, and ham, and another plate covered by a mattress-sized cinnamon roll.

Mother gave the first genuine smile in a couple of days and said, "I remember when I could eat like that and not gain an ounce."

"I think we can all afford a few extra calories after the diet we've been on this week."

There was very little talk after that, until, one by one, we pushed our plates away and sank into satisfied stupor. I paid the bill, relishing the ease of using my debit card, while Kurt glanced over a newspaper to see if we had missed any earth-shaking events in the last few days.

The sun was breaking through when we got outside, and we stood for a few minutes talking about our plans for the rest of the trip.

"Our adventures have thrown a monkey wrench in the itinerary I planned. I expected we would be halfway through Oklahoma by now. We still have over 500 miles to go. We could do it by tomorrow night but I'd rather not." Kurt ran his hand through his hair and looked at me. "What day did you tell them we would be there?"

I grimaced. "Tomorrow. But their show doesn't start until Wednesday."

"Maybe you should call them and tell them we'll shoot for Monday."

"I don't think that'll be a problem. I'll call them now." I dug in my purse for my phone and the number of Johnny Norton's dealership.

While I was on the phone, Kurt got out the atlas and opened it on the hood of the Jeep.

As I put my phone away, Kurt said, "Well? What's the verdict?"

"They're fine with end of business Monday. They would like us to stay around for the opening of the exhibit on Wednesday because they've got a local camera crew coming in to do interviews."

Dinah's head snapped up. "We're going to be on TV?"

"Just an Amarillo local station," I said. "Not network prime-time, exactly."

"Okay, here's a suggestion. Springfield for lunch. It's isn't far but there's a couple of stops I'd like to make between here and there. Then it's about three hours to Tulsa and we find a motel there tonight. One with hot showers." He grinned and sniffed an armpit, making a face. "Tomorrow on to Oklahoma City, some site-seeing there and go as far as Weatherford, Oklahoma tomorrow night. That would leave us with about a three hour run into Amarillo on Monday. Plenty of time to deliver the trailer and find a place to stay."

"Are we going to see the Oklahoma City Memorial?" Mother asked.

"That's a must," Kurt said.

"Sounds good to me." I said. "What sights are between here and Springfield?"

"The Munger Moss Motel in Lebanon is pretty much a must see. And Dinah, there's a puzzle store at Lebanon with thousands of puzzles."

"Sweet," she said. High Praise.

We loaded back into the Jeep, more relaxed than when we had started this trip almost a week before. The road traversed more gentle hills, and the forest had been pushed back to allow for homes, farms, and small businesses. We passed remnants of 'tourist courts' — much cuter and more welcoming than today's mega chain hotels. Playhouse-looking cottages clustered randomly around weed invested parking lots. Most had been white at one time, with blue or green or red roofs, and in spite of the ravages of time, they invited exploration. Perhaps that attraction is connected to the appeal of the tiny house movement in our own time.

Sixty-six dipped south away from I-44 and then swung back to meet the interstate right after Gascozark— a wonderful name actually applied to the whole area and derived by marrying Ozark and the name of the nearby Gasconade River. The ruins of a trading post with the same name sat near the interstate.

We then followed a frontage road that paralleled the Interstate and were soon back into hillier country. The road crossed the Gasconade River on a steel bridge from the 1920s.

We commented from time to time on the relics of the past scattered along the roadside. Old neon signs, tumble-down brick store fronts, or an occasional rusted out truck had us speculating about what happened there at one time. It made me think of perusing a recent family photo album in which someone had used old Polaroid or black-and-white snapshots to bookmark certain pages. The scenery was mostly familiar, but broken by glimpses of things that were vaguely recognizable in the same way that an ancestor could be identified by a unique hairline or shape of chin.

I think we were all relieved to have only mundane topics to think about or discuss. No awkward questions today.

We reached Lebanon and pulled in at the Munger Moss Motel. Kurt informed us that this was its 70th year of operation, having been built in 1946. The gift shop offered a variety of Route 66 memorabilia—from tacky spoon holders, dishtowels, and shot glasses to framed drawings and watercolors done by local artists.

After visiting with the owner, we drove a couple of blocks to Wrink's Market, another business that had been around since the middle of the last century. The market itself was not currently open, but Decker's Cowboy Emporium was and included a small restaurant and western museum in part of the building. We each had one of Decker's fried pies and spent an hour admiring the collection of art and artifacts from the Old West culture.

Finally, Kurt prodded us. "There's two other things we need to see here. There's a Route 66 museum at the library and the puzzle place." He looked at Dinah. She gave a fist pump, and we exited the building.

The library museum was like a movie set, with a black-and-white checked floor, replicas of a diner and a vintage gas station, a collection of salt and pepper shakers from Route 66 and even a vintage car. An old telephone switchboard led to questions from Dinah about just picking up a phone and talking to an operator, as we had experienced in the Fifties.

We snapped Dinah's and Mother's pictures hamming it up on the soda fountain stools as pinup girls, ala Betty

Grable or Lana Turner. Dinah picked out a 1949 Packard from an old photo that she thought she ought to have. We decided it was time to move on to the puzzle store.

Dinah insisted since she wasn't getting a vintage car, she deserved at least a puzzle and picked out one with a Route 66 theme. Kurt, possibly thinking of that hot shower, herded us out the door and back into the Jeep.

The Lebanon to Springfield section was more of what we had seen in the morning, except the road was generally straighter, and there were more open pastures and small fields of corn. We weren't very hungry but were still ready to get out at Springfield at another Mom-and-Pop restaurant.

CHAPTER TWENTY ONE

Lynne

AT LUNCH, WE BOOED DOWN Kurt's suggestion to visit the Missouri Sports Hall of Fame before we left town, but did consider the Air and Military Museum a possibility. Dinah thought we definitely should add the local chocolate factory tour.

Kurt shook his head. "Those sound like lengthy stops. Here's an assignment for you, Dinah. Find a blank page in your little notebook, and write down the places we don't think we have time for on the way down and where they are. We can certainly hit at least some of them on the way back. Today, we'll only stop at places that won't take long."

"That's cool." She pulled a little spiral notebook out of her purse and grinned like the Cheshire Cat. "And if it's somewhere I don't want to stop, I can 'forget' to write it down."

"I'll supervise her and make sure she gets everything," Mother said.

"Aw, Grandma."

IN KEEPING WITH THAT PLAN, we headed out of Springfield and followed an early version of the Mother Road past towns nearly abandoned with names like Albatross and Phelps. In Carthage, Dinah added the Phelps House and the Powers Museum to the list and we drove by the Boots Motel where Clark Gable once stayed.

In Joplin, Mother made her write down the Thomas Hart Benton Museum. Kurt told her to be sure to add Grand Falls. Mother reported that Dinah included another candy store as well.

We left Missouri and cut through the southeast corner of Kansas, an area once economically dependent on mining, now converted to recreational uses. We made no stops, but Kurt insisted that when we came back, we would make a side trip to see 'Big Brutus', a sixteen-story high power shovel.

As we entered Oklahoma, Kurt explained that a direct route from Chicago to Los Angeles would have by passed Oklahoma entirely and gone through Kansas instead. But an influential Oklahoman who served on the Joint Board determining the route saw this as an opportunity to bring his home state, only a decade old at the time, into the nation's consciousness. He did not foresee that ten years later during the depths of the depression, many "Okies" would be using the Mother Road to flee to California.

On we motored toward Tulsa. Kurt instructed Dinah to write down both a motorcycle and a hot rod museum — research, he said — and we also added a couple of Civil War sites. A side trip in Foyil snagged us the double whammy of a stop at the Top Hat Dairy Bar and a view of Totem Pole Park.

Kurt suggested a downtown Tulsa hotel so that we could use the late afternoon and evening hours to visit some historical sites and curiosities. In the latter category, Dinah insisted on the Center of the Universe. If we were honest, the adults would have admitted that we were intrigued too. It is an acoustical anomaly, allowing a visitor to stand in the center and make any sound which will come reverberating back louder than the original. On our way downtown, Kurt took us by the Golden Driller, a 75-foot statue at the International Petroleum Exposition.

The next day continued like the previous one: few stops, Dinah making hurried notes about what we want to come back to, no kidnappings, no arrests — in short, the great American road trip. Except for making sure we only ate lunch at tables with a view of the parking lot and checking the door locks on the camper at least three times every stop. Kurt was able to find a hotel in Tulsa with a security guard at the parking ramp, As we left town the next day, he stopped at a Best Buy and bought a tracking device to put in the camper. Just in case.

The highlight, I think, for all of us was the Oklahoma City National Monument—a somber reminder of the deadly terrorist attack on the Murrah Building twenty-one years earlier. Dinah was so moved by the empty chairs that she suggested that we could go back to 1995 and warn people. This began a long discussion about how you could possibly convince people that the attack was going to occur and how many tragedies could you prevent and what would be the effects on time since then and on and on. It actually was a good discussion to vent our frustrations and bring some of our concerns out in the open.

Before Oklahoma City, we had made a brief stop at POPS, a 66-foot lighted pop bottle where you could choose from a wide variety of soft drinks. Kurt also instructed Dinah to add the Blue Bell Saloon in Guthrie to the list where Tom Mix once tended bar and gunfights are reenacted outside.

We spent the night at Weatherford and continued on the last short leg to Texas. There were more historical and hot rod museums added to the list. My favorite stop, however, was the Alanreed Travel Center shortly after we crossed in to Texas. Gifts, toys, wine, a post office, clothes —all in a space not much bigger than the average garage. But, the high point of the day was crossing the city limits into Amarillo.

CHAPTER TWENTY-TWO
Edna Mae

EDNA MAE BARKER was feeling every minute of her ninety-four years. She was tempted to stay in bed, but her granddaughter Kim was coming this morning, probably to deliver a lecture on her eating habits and attempt one more time to talk her into assisted living.

She loved her children and grandchildren fiercely (and great-grandchildren, although she didn't know any of them very well), but why couldn't they leave well enough alone? She also loved her little house, where she had a great view of Texas sunrises and sunsets. The modifications her son had done years ago made it comfortable and workable for her.

She pushed herself to a sitting position and worked her way to her feet. She did a little gentle stretching — low impact, they called it — and managed to get her clothes on. She slipped her feet into her fuzzy slippers and padded out to her kitchen to plug in her coffee pot. Her doctor said she drank too much caffeine, but she just scoffed at him. What was it going to do, shorten her life? She ought to take up smoking. That would show him.

In the living room, she turned to a news channel on the TV and settled in her platform rocker. After a few minutes, she decided the news was too depressing, clicked it off, and picked up her latest Michael Connelly book, *The Crossing*. Time to see what Harry Bosch was up to.

A half hour later, she heard the porch door open, and Kim's voice through the inside screen.

"Grandma? Why is your door open? Don't you have the air on?" Kim breezed in and kissed Edna Mae on the top of her head.

"Not yet, dear. It's not that hot, and I love to have the windows open. Have a seat. Do you want some coffee?"

Kim sat on the couch. "Nope—already had my two cups for today. How are you feeling this morning?"

"Just fine."

Kim was an attractive 46-year-old teacher, and during the summer, she came to visit Edna Mae two or three times a week. Edna Mae knew she meant well and loved to see her.

Kim sat forward. "Well, I have a plan."

Oh-oh, Edna Mae thought. *Here we go again.* "And what is that?"

"There's an antique camper show going on over at

Johnny Norton's museum. I thought if you feel up to it, we should go check it out. Then we could go out for lunch."

Edna Mae was surprised, but she frowned. "You know I don't like that fellow."

Kim laughed. "Grandma, you can't fault him for owning part of your farm. You put it up for sale, and he paid your asking price. He's a nice guy."

"That land should still be in the family. What's this show about?" Edna Mae decided she should encourage Kim as long as she wasn't pushing the nursing home.

"Old campers. Johnny has a lot of them in his museum, but he borrowed some others for this show, and there's a vintage camper rally going on in his parking lot at the same time. I thought they would be fun to look at. Didn't you and Grandpa have a camper once?"

Edna Mae nodded. "When we were first married. I sold it after he didn't come back from the war." She could never say *he died* or *he was killed*—just that he didn't come back. Kim of course, was born long after, but since Edna Mae talked about Cal Barker like he was still around, the kids all felt they knew him.

"Are you up for it? I called, and they have a wheel chair there we can borrow."

Edna Mae sputtered. "I don't need a wheel chair. My cane will do just fine."

"Whatever," Kim said.

"I'll drive," Edna Mae said.

185

Kim shook her head. "Not today. You are ninety-four, you know."

"I have a license."

"That doesn't mean you *should* be driving." Kim smiled at her as she opened the passenger door of her red compact and helped her in.

SINCE IT WAS A WEEKDAY, the crowd was small. They moved slowly around the parking lot, peeking in old Shastas, Serro Scottys, and Airstreams. The day was warming up, and Kim noticed Edna Mae moved slower the farther they went.

"Shall we go inside? I think there's refreshments." Kim winked at her. They went inside the RV showroom that was Johnny Norton's business. The museum in the back was his hobby. A table offered tea, lemonade, and chocolate chip cookies. Several folding chairs sat nearby.

"Let's sit a bit," Edna said.

"Sure. Are you rethinking that wheel chair maybe? We could take your cane along, and you can get up and walk when you want to."

"Mebbe," Edna Mae said, around a mouthful of cookie.

It was settled. After their cookies and lemonade, Kim asked about the wheelchair at the main desk. A young man, with "Chad" embroidered above his shirt pocket, brought one out from a closet, twirled it around in front of Edna Mae, did a wheelie, and then bowed to her. Edna

Mae clapped and said to Kim, "I want him to push me."

Kim laughed and said, "Grandma, remember you promised no flirting."

The young man helped Edna Mae into the chair and kissed her on the cheek. As Kim pushed her toward the back door and the museum, she said, "I do believe you're blushing."

"Posh!" said Edna Mae.

"Have you ever been here before?"

"No."

"Because you're mad about the land?"

"Mebbe."

They stopped first in front of an old truck from the early Twentieth Century that had a tent that popped out of the back.

Edna Mae said, "That's too much roughing it for me."

Each display had a story board with the make and the year, the history of that particular camper, and accessories arranged on large pieces of artificial grass.

"Oooh," Edna Mae said. "Look at that green metal ice chest. My dad had one like that. And on that picnic table —see the Parcheesi game? We used to play that all the time."

At each display, Kim held the chair steady so Edna could stand up and walk to the door of the camper or tent. She didn't want to tackle the steps, but she would lean in as far as she could and look around. Many of the items—calendars, enamel coffee pots, flowered dishes, checked curtains—reminded her of her childhood or early years as Cal's bride. Even old Tones spice cans and Bakelite radios brought back sweet memories. She had to dig in a pocket of her velour sweat suit for a tissue several times to wipe her eyes.

"Are you okay?" Kim asked once when she returned to the wheelchair.

"Yes." Edna Mae looked up at her granddaughter. "This is very nice. It was sweet of you to think of me."

Kim hugged her. "We have several more to see and then—lunch! We'll go to that place that has the really good fried chicken." Kim was having a little trouble with her own eyes.

She rolled the chair into the next room and they looked first at a vintage Winnebago motorhome. Edna Mae got back in the chair, and Kim rolled her around the front of the big RV to the next exhibit—an old trailer.

Edna Mae gasped.

Kim bent over her with concern. "Are you okay? Do you need water or something?"

Her grandmother shook her head and pointed at the old trailer. "We had one just like that—your grandpa and I. It's a Covered Wagon, made in Michigan."

"Really?" Kim said. "What a coincidence!"

"Not really. They made more trailers in the Thirties than any other company. Here, help me up, please."

Kim did, and Edna Mae almost giggled as Kim guided her to the door. Kim was afraid she would trip in her excitement and fall.

The trailer was brown with a white roof. Edna Mae trailed her hand along the side. "They covered these with leatherette—kind of like vinyl. And the roof is canvas that has been sealed."

"Do you want to see inside?"

"Yes. I'm going to go inside. I can make it up two steps."

She could, but it wasn't easy, even with Kim's help. Once inside, she sat on the couch. Kim noticed a small sign asking people not to sit on the furniture, but decided her bird-like grandmother didn't weigh enough to make a difference.

"Is this what yours was like?"

"Oh, yes. Well, there was different fabric on the cushions and of course different curtains." Edna Mae touched one of the curtains. "I think someone made these out of old aprons." Tears ran down her cheeks. "We had such wonderful times in this, Kim. If only I had known then how little time I would have with Cal."

Kim said softly, "Where did you go in it?"

"Sometimes we just camped on the farm. Other times we would go down to Palo Duro Canyon. It was a new state park then."

"Sounds wonderful."

"Your mom was just a baby. It was a hassle with diapers and bottles, but we made do. Such a special time. After your uncle David was born, we only went once or twice before your grandpa got drafted." Edna Mae shook her head and pushed herself to her feet. "We'd better go." She squeezed Kim's hand. "This was so special. I get such a feeling of peace here."

Kim helped her down the steps. But Edna Mae wasn't ready to leave. She stood back and stared at the trailer as others came and went. She mentioned to several people that she had once owned a camper like that one.

CHAPTER TWENTY-THREE
Lynne

IT WAS A HUGE RELIEF to arrive at Johnny Norton's dealership on the south side of Amarillo and unhook the camper. Mr. Norton was a small man who exuded enthusiasm for his chosen sales area. After we introduced ourselves and made small talk about our trip down—the condensed version—he followed us out to look at the trailer.

He clapped his hands and grinned from ear to ear. "This is wonderful! And you did all of the restoration?"

"Lynne did," Kurt said. "I thought she was crazy."

Better not go there.

"Fantastic! Are you going to be able to stick around until Wednesday for the TV interview? They'll want to know what all you did with it. If that won't work, I might be able to get them out here tomorrow."

"That's not necessary," I said. "There's several sites we want to take in around here. Wednesday will be fine."

WE FOUND A NEARBY MOTEL and reserved two nights. Dinah delighted in the outdoor pool and even more in the presence of several other teenagers. She flirted with the boys and giggled with the girls. Mother and I basked in the sun until it got too warm, and Kurt installed himself on one of the beds in our room, the TV remote firmly gripped in his hand. It was a much needed respite from the stress of our travels.

ON TUESDAY, WE DROVE down to Palo Duro Canyon, touted in the brochure as surpassed in size only by the Grand Canyon. We drove down into the canyon, stopped at pull offs to photograph the amazing colored rock formations and take short hikes on a couple of the trails. The Visitor Center provided spectacular views and a wonderful display of Native American art.

We returned to Amarillo and drove along several old sections of 66. Of course, we had to take in the Cadillac Ranch and the Floating Mesa, both creations of the eccentric businessman, Stanley Marsh 3. (Another of his eccentricities was using an Arabic rather than Roman numeral after his name.) The Big Texan Steak Ranch provided supper and a fine finish to the day. By that time, Dinah was anxious to return to the motel, the pool, and hopefully, her new friends.

THE NEXT MORNING, after assuring Dinah that the hour spent on her makeup and hair had achieved matchless results, we returned as requested to the RV dealership at 8:30 for our TV debut. The local newsman interviewed us both outside and inside the camper. Johnny Norton had arranged artificial grass and various vintage camping paraphernalia around the trailer, and one segment focused on Dinah in her 1950s' dress, lounging in a metal lawn chair.

The night before, we had discussed at length what we could say in the interview without being hauled off to the loony bin. I was confident that Dinah would not burst out with "Yeah, it's way live — we time-travel in it!"

After the interview, Dinah went to the restroom to change into something more 2016, and we walked through the rest of the exhibits. It was exciting to be a part of such a slice of Americana. Dinah rejoined us, and we went out to see the vintage campers displayed in the parking lot.

Back inside, we made one more pass to check out people's reactions to our Covered Wagon. We felt a little like stalkers as we eavesdropped on comments. One elderly woman stood back a bit and I could see tears in her eyes. She leaned on a cane with her other hand through the arm of a younger, attractive dark-haired woman.

Curious, I moved nearer to her.

She turned to me suddenly and said, "My husband and I used to have one exactly like that."

Probably not exactly like it.

"Really?" I said. "When was that?"

"The early Forties. But he didn't come back from the War so I sold it. We had wonderful times in it."

Didn't come back? Did he die or leave her? I didn't want to ask.

"This one belongs to us. We bought it from a friend."

She peered into my face. "Y'all don't sound like you're from Texas."

"We're from Iowa. We brought this down Monday for this exhibit."

"Thank you." She removed her hand from the other woman's arm and held it out. "I'm Edna Mae Barker and this is my granddaughter Kim."

"How nice to meet you. So obviously you have children. Did you remarry?"

"Never. My Rose Ann, Kim's mother, was just a toddler and Davey was eight months old when Cal was drafted."

My family joined us so I introduced them.

"Did you camp in it a lot?" Kurt asked.

"Sometimes just on our farm, but my favorite trips were to Palo Duro Canyon. That was the farthest we went."

Dinah jumped in. "We went there yesterday. It's so beautiful!"

"Yes, it is, dear." Edna Mae then leaned over to me and whispered, "No one else was here when we got here this morning, so I went it inside and sat for a few minutes. It was like having my Cal back." Tears gathered in her eyes again.

I still held her hand. It was cool and papery. "I'm glad it means so much to you. That makes it worth bringing it down here." I caught a sharp glance from my mother.

She let go of my hand and took a few careful steps closer the camper. I had the feeling she was worshipping at an altar.

"This means so much to her," Kim said.

"I can see that. Did her husband—your grandfather? —die in the war? She said 'he didn't come back.'"

"Yes, he was killed in Normandy. But she always says that. I don't think she's given up on him returning." Kim gave a soft smile and she, too, had teary eyes.

Edna Mae came back and shook my hand. "Thank you again. You can't imagine what this means to me. Are you interested in selling it?"

"I don't think so," I said.

Kim laughed. "You may still be able to drive, Grandma, but I seriously doubt if you are up to towing a camper. No offense."

"Of course not. I would just sit in it and think about the old days."

Kim had pulled a wheel chair over. "It's time for lunch. Think about that chicken!" She got Edna Mae settled in the chair with her cane in her lap, and turned to us. "So nice to meet you. Safe travels back home."

We said our goodbyes, and off they went.

Kurt said, "That was certainly a fitting end to this trip." I could swear that he looked a little weepy. "I think it's time we got on the road and get started on Dinah's list."

I took one last look at the little trailer that had brought us such adventures—scary and otherwise.

Mother said, "You made it sound like it was a breeze bringing it down here."

She hadn't mentioned Verl James the last two days, but obviously he was still on her mind.

Kurt said, "I know that experience was awful, Linda, and will probably be a burden for you for a long time to come. But we should all remember that Lynne was never in favor of the time travel. She went along with it to please us."

Mom looked at me sadly and took my hand. "He's right. I'm so sorry. Will you forgive me?"

We still had our arms around each other when we reached the Jeep.

CHAPTER TWENTY-FOUR
Edna Mae

DURING THE NEXT SEVERAL DAYS, Edna Mae often thought about the trailer. She would be on her porch in the rocker with her book, and suddenly find herself staring out at the Texas fields, thinking about the old Covered Wagon. It made her miss Cal even more.

The following Saturday, after doing her dishes and dusting the living room furniture — that cleaning woman the kids had hired for her was pleasant and a hard worker, but she really didn't know how to dust — she decided she would go back to Johnny Norton's. After all, it wasn't far to drive. The RV dealership bordered what remained of her farm.

She washed her face and combed her hair. Thank goodness the kids had put in a garage door opener. That was a task she probably couldn't do any more. It took her a while to walk to the garage, get the door open, and get in the car, but she had time. The museum was open until 5:00.

When she got there, the parking lot was full with the weekend visitors so she parked on a side street. Her cane helped her across the rough ground to the front gate. When she finally got inside, she was surprised at the crowd and the noise. However, she knew where she wanted to go. Most people noticed her frailty and stepped aside so that she could get through the crowd.

Back in the museum, she went directly to the old trailer. A little park bench sat between it and the Winnebago where she could rest from her long walk. She sat there for an hour, occasionally visited with others, but usually just stared at the camper, lost in time.

Cal had worked for the Civilian Conservation Corps before they were married and had built up a little savings account. His father had died and his mother turned the farm over to him. It was the middle of the depression and prices were terrible, but they could grow their own food and they managed to hang on. One day after their marriage, he came home, towing the trailer behind his old pickup.

She fell in love with it immediately, but thought it was very foolish. "Cal, how can we possibly afford this?"

He looked kind of sheepish. "I took a little money out of our savings. It was repossessed by the bank, and they didn't want much for it." He put his arm around her. "When we got married, I promised I would take you away, and we would travel the world. Of course that hasn't worked out, but this way we can travel our own little world."

They did just that. They didn't go far, but Cal found some lovely spots for weekend trips. When little Rose Ann—Rosie—came along, Cal fixed up a laundry basket as a bed for her. It was wonderful.

"Ma'am? Do you mind if I sit here?" An older man—well, not older than Edna Mae—interrupted her daydreams. She slid over a little.

"No, not at all. Silly of me to take up the whole bench."

"I just didn't want to bother you. You looked like you were in another world."

She smiled. "Another time perhaps."

He leaned back and set his cap on his knee. "These antiques will do that. Wonderful exhibit."

"Yes, it is. Were you a camper?"

"Still am. I have a van that I travel all over with. I'm from Tennessee—Nashville."

"How nice. You mean you're on the road full time?"

"Yup. Stayin' down at Palo Duro Canyon this week."

Edna Mae smiled. "My husband and I used to camp there. It's beautiful. We had a trailer just like that one."

"How long ago was that?"

"The Thirties and Forties. He didn't come back from the war."

He covered her hand with his. "I'm sorry about that.

It's been very nice meeting you, but I have to go find a grocery store before I go back to the park."

"Have a wonderful trip," she said, and went back to her dreams.

The crowd was thinning out, and she looked at her watch. It was getting close to 5:00. She had felt peaceful and secure when she was sitting in that trailer the other day, and she had made a plan. The dealer was not open on Sundays, and Edna Mae decided that if she hid in the camper on Saturday night, she could spend a whole day wrapped in that feeling. There was a restroom and drinking fountain in the museum, and she had brought her toothbrush, a flashlight, and a change of underwear. She could sleep on the couch. Rosie and David didn't usually visit on Sunday because their grandchildren were so involved in sports. It would be her little vacation.

She walked over to the camper door and waited until there was no one in that room of the museum. Then she carefully climbed the two steps into the camper. There was a rope across the end where the kitchen and dinette were. She unhooked the loop, stepped past it and hooked it up again. She sat at the dinette holding her purse. If Kim or any of the others knew what she was doing, they would put her in the home for sure.

The museum was getting very quiet and, although her hearing wasn't too great any more, a man's shout of "Anybody here?" came through loud and clear. She pulled back from the windows in case he came around to check. She wasn't worried; if they caught her, she would just play the 'demented old lady' card.

The lights dimmed outside the windows, and she heard a big door slam shut.

Edna Mae relaxed and soaked up the atmosphere in the camper. She felt closer to Cal here than anywhere else — even their home. She lay her head back. Cal was so handsome. She pictured him coming in from the fields on a summer day, his light brown hair wind-blown and his freckles brought out by the sun. He would push his straw hat back from his forehead and give her a kiss. His eyes were as blue as the Texas sky. Then she pictured him as he looked in 1942 before he shipped overseas. He wore his cap at a jaunty angle, and his army uniform showed off his farm boy muscles.

The only thing she saw of him after that was a flag-draped coffin.

She was crying again. She sat up, wiped her eyes, and pulled a sandwich and a bottle of water out of her purse. She would pretend she and Cal were having lunch together in the camper. Except for the plastic taste of that bottled water. They had fresh well water back then.

Kim had given her an ereader the Christmas before that had a backlight in it, so she could sit at the table and read without using up her flashlight. She liked hard cover books better, but there were times like this when the ereader was handy.

Soon, however, she felt very stiff from sitting at the

little table. She looked at her watch. It was almost eight o'clock. Many evenings she went to bed about that time. She got her flashlight, worked her way down the steps, and over to the nearby restroom. By the time she got back, another half hour had gone, and it was bedtime.

She hadn't been able to figure out a way to bring in a blanket or a pillow. She opened and searched the cabinets. The owners actually had quite a few things in them: a few dishes, some clothes, a couple of towels, pillows and blankets, and some old license plates. That was odd. But she was in luck and made up a bed on the couch with a pillow and a blanket.

She lay down and pulled the blanket around her, staring into the dark. The last thing she was conscious of was her simple wedding band. As she caressed it, she dropped off to sleep.

CHAPTER TWENTY-FIVE
Edna Mae

WHEN EDNA MAE WOKE UP, she lay as she usually did, dreading getting out of bed and moving around before her muscles loosened up. Then she remembered where she was.

But light was streaming in the trailer windows. That wasn't right—the museum was supposed to be closed on Sunday. She sat up. Something else odd—she didn't hurt. She looked down at her hands—smooth and browned by the sun. And she was wearing a blue cotton dress. When she looked outside, fields stretched in every direction. It was daylight but the cloudless sky had a funny yellow cast.

She knew she was dreaming. She remembered that sky—the dust hung so thick that no blue could penetrate. Several years of drought had plagued the plains and the land blew away.

She left the trailer, easily descended the steps, and walked quickly down the dirt road, no cane needed. She could see her house. Now it needed paint and the big shade trees weren't there yet. When she got to the house, she knocked on the back door and then thought: how silly. Did she expect herself to open the door? Cal's truck was gone so he wasn't going to answer. She went in. They had never locked the door—there was nothing to steal.

She looked at the calendar over the kitchen sink—June, 1939. She and Cal had only been married a few months. There were dishes piled in the sink. She grabbed the apron off a hook on the wall and tied it around her waist. She noticed how slim her waist and flat her stomach was. Funny—she always thought she was kind of chubby when they got married.

She pumped water in a pan and put it on the stove to heat. Tasks that she had not done for decades came as easily and naturally as if she still did them every day. Strange.

When she finished the dishes, she hung up the apron and went out on the front porch to wait for Cal on the swing. It was hot and her mouth felt gritty, and she went back in to pump a glass of water. The glass was decorated with red and yellow flowers, part of a set they had received as a wedding gift. The kitchen curtains were red and yellow too. She had made them out of flour sacks and was proud of them—so bright and fresh. Now they hung dingy from the dust after only a couple of months.

Back on the swing, she kept her eyes on the road to town, watching for the telltale cloud of dust that would mean Cal was headed home. She probably had work to do, but she was tired and a little scared. What did this all mean?

She must have dozed, because the next thing she knew, Cal's truck was pulling in the farmyard. Could you nap in a dream? She didn't know but couldn't think about it. She saw his lanky form descend from the truck and her heart pounded. She jumped out of the swing and ran toward him.

Cal grinned when he saw her coming and put down the bag of feed he was unloading. He picked her up and swung her around, smothering her with a long kiss.

"What brought that on, darlin'?" he said as he set her down. "Not that I'm complainin'."

"I just missed you," she said.

"Good." He picked the bag up again and hefted it over his shoulder. "Any coffee left?"

"I—don't know." She didn't notice a coffee pot in the kitchen. "I'll check." She rushed back into the house. By the time, he came into the house, she had a pot brewing on the stove.

He sat down at the table, and she filled a mug for him. She also set the sugar bowl and a spoon near him. Funny how she could remember some things but not others.

She sat across from him and leaned her elbows on the table. "Any news from town?"

He grew serious. "More people leavin.' Farmers mostly but some businesses. Things ain't improving much with this drought."

"What will we do?"

"I don't know. Without rain, we're gonna lose this crop. Maybe I should enlist."

"What? What would I do?"

"You could go back and live with your parents. I could bank my pay..."

"No! What if there's war?"

"Then I'd probably have to go anyway."

She couldn't let this happen. She remembered this fight. She had to hold her ground. He got up.

"Got work to do. We'll talk about this later."

She changed the subject. "Gonna be really hot today. Maybe we could catch a swim later in the pond. Remember how we used to do that?" She touched his arm.

He narrowed his eyes at her. "There ain't been water in that pond since I've known you."

"Oh." She blushed. "Must have been a dream."

"I guess." He gave her a quick kiss on the forehead, put his coffee mug by the sink, and was out the door.

She busied herself the rest of the morning with household tasks. There was laundry to do and dust on the furniture. Always dust on the furniture. Then she remembered lunch. Cal needed a big lunch in the middle of his strenuous day. Not just sandwiches. She fried up a piece of ham and sliced two potatoes. There was a pie and a loaf of bread in the cupboard, and she cut him a big slice of each.

While she waited for him to come in, she pumped a little water in her hands and splashed it on her face. For a few minutes, she would feel fresh. She'd forgotten how precious the water was. She thought wistfully of the air conditioning she would have in this house later in her life. They had only just gotten electricity in 1939.

After lunch, they sat on the porch, fanning themselves in the hot wind and pretending it was a cool breeze. Cal had brought a newspaper home from town. It was the previous day's issue that he picked up free at the coffee shop but it provided a little connection to the world. Not that there was much good news.

They moved inside, and for a while it felt almost cool. They kept the house closed during the day and the curtains drawn to keep out the heat and the dust. Cal read the paper and then dozed in his chair. He would go back out later in the afternoon when the temperature dropped slightly.

Edna Mae went back to the kitchen to plan a supper. She would make gravy with the left over ham and they would have it on corn bread. She got a jar of applesauce out of the pantry. The shelves were getting bare and, from the looks of the meager offerings in her kitchen garden, there wouldn't be much to put up this fall either.

Cal came up behind her as she stared out the window and wrapped his arms around her. "We need to talk, honey," he whispered. He took her hand and pulled her back into the living room. They sat side by side on the couch and she picked at her skirt.

"I don't want to leave you," he began. "God knows I don't. But we're gonna have nothing to buy seed with for next year. I can sell off the livestock, and since we've got no mortgage, we can just let the farm sit."

She shook her head and tears ran down her face.

"No! No! We just got married, Cal. I can't lose you."

"You won't lose me. Maybe I'll be stationed here in Texas and you can visit me." He grinned that boyish smile that twisted her heart. "Those would be some visits."

She didn't smile.

"We have to get some money somehow. The only other thing we can do is sell the farm and move to California."

But they both knew no one was buying farms.

"Wait a little longer," she said. "Maybe it'll rain."

He shook his head. "We can't wait any longer." His voice became firmer. "Edna Mae, we've talked about this until I'm blue in the face. It is what it is. Tomorrow, I'm going in to the enlistment office, and you need to talk to your parents about moving in with them. Maybe you can get a job. That would help." He got up. "Time for me to get back out there and finish some things up. I'm bringing the machinery in—I might be able to sell some of it."

He was gone.

She sat and sobbed. Then she got mad. She picked up a little figurine from the end table and threw it across the room against the wall. He couldn't do this to her. What about those marriage vows? He had promised to take care of her, and how could he do that if he left her? She picked up the pieces of the figurine to throw them away. The head of the little French shepherdess was still intact. That made her cry harder, and she stuck it in her pocket.

She stormed out of the house and down the road to the little trailer. It was hidden from the house by a clutch of scrubby trees. When she reached the trailer, she slammed and locked the door. The more she cried, the more her anger grew. She twisted her wedding ring off and threw it across the trailer. Then she collapsed on the couch-bed and cried herself to sleep.

CHAPTER TWENTY-SIX
Edna Mae

EDNA MAE WOKE in the morning, her body awash with aches and pains. It was early and still dark. She looked out the window. A security light cast a dim glow through out the museum. She was back. What a dream—it seemed so real. But was it Sunday or Monday morning? She remembered her cell phone and took it out of her handbag.

It was Monday. The museum and dealership would be opening soon. Edna Mae went out of the camper to use the restroom and brush her teeth. She planned to come back and hide in the restroom at opening time, wait a bit and then come out and pretend she had just come in that morning.

But first she straightened up the trailer, put the blanket and pillow away, and collected all of her belongings into her bag. She sat down to wait until closer to opening time and think about her experience. How could she have slept through a whole day without waking once? She shifted and felt a lump in her pocket. It was the head of the shepherdess. How could she have something from a dream?

She remembered that argument with Cal and what happened afterwards. He did go to town the next day to enlist, but saw a sign looking for construction workers to help build the new Veterans' Hospital. He was able to get a job, and rains during the fall brought an end to the drought. Their fortunes picked up as farm prices improved, Rosie was born the next year, and Cal bought their trailer.

She sighed and looked around the little camper one last time. A glint from under the table caught her eye. Her wedding ring! How lucky was she to find that before she left. She put it back on and returned to the restroom.

SHE WANDERED AROUND THE MUSEUM a little after it opened. The story board in front of the Covered Wagon listed the museum in Illinois that it was borrowed from and the names of the owners. She got out her little notepad and wrote them down.

It was time to get back home and have a bath and a decent meal. Kim texted her to see how she was doing and said she would probably stop by late in the afternoon. Edna Mae left the museum, went to her car on the side street, and drove home.

That afternoon, she sat down with her smartphone that she was slowly learning to use and typed in the name of the Illinois museum to get the phone number. Herb Branson, the owner answered, and Edna Mae explained her interest in the camper. Mr. Branson told her the owners were not interested in selling, but he gave her their phone number anyway.

Edna Mae then tried the number for Kurt and Lynne McBriar but only got voice mail. She tried to leave a message that would interest them and not scare them off.

"Hello, Mr. and Mrs. McBriar. This is Edna Mae Barker and I met you when you brought your trailer to Amarillo. I just wanted to tell you again how much I enjoyed seeing your Covered Wagon. If you have time to call me back, I have some questions. Thank you."

Kim stopped by that afternoon and brought her a bowl of chicken pasta salad for her supper. The weather had cooled a little and they sat on the porch visiting about Kim's children and the local gossip. After Kim left, Edna Mae took a plate of the pasta out to the porch to enjoy the evening. She had just finished when her cell phone rang. It was Lynne McBriar.

Edna Mae said, "Can I ask why you don't use it any more? Why did you put it in a museum?"

Lynne hesitated. "Our daughter is a teenager, and we are so busy with her activities that we really don't have time to camp. We didn't want it to just sit."

Edna Mae laughed. "Oh, yes, I remember those years.

Well, I just love it. When I go in it, I feel so close to my husband Cal."

"I could tell that it was very special to you."

"I have another question. When you camped in it, did you ever have anything odd happen?"

There was a long silence. Edna Mae said, "Mrs. McBriar? Are you still there?"

"Yes. I'm sorry. What do you mean, odd?"

"Well, I have a confession. Like I said, I like to sit in there and feel close to my husband. And last Saturday I fell asleep and spent the night in it." She heard a gasp from the other end of the line. "I had the strangest dream that I went back in time to 1939 and saw my husband again."

Another long silence. "That is odd. Mrs. Barker, can I call you back in a little bit? Uh, someone's at my door."

"Certainly, dear. I would like to talk to you more, because I would really like to buy that camper."

"Uh, yes, I'll explain that when I call back."

They said good-bye. Edna Mae rocked and watched the western sky.

ABOUT AN HOUR LATER, the phone rang again.

Lynne McBriar said, "Mrs. Barker? I hope it's not too late."

"Not at all," Edna Mae said.

"This is very difficult, but after your experience I feel I have some explaining to do. I don't think you had a dream. That camper time travels." She paused. "I wouldn't expect you to believe it, except that you've experienced it."

Edna Mae didn't say anything.

"We put the trailer in a museum because we have had several rather bad experiences with it. We decided not to sell it because the new owner might have the same thing."

Lynne went on to explain how they thought the remodeling had something to do with it as well as jewelry from the time. "Mrs. Barker, were you wearing anything from 1939 when you fell asleep?"

Edna Mae thought a few seconds. "My wedding ring."

"But didn't you still have it on when you came back to the present or woke up?"

"No, I didn't. In my dream, I had an argument with my husband. Because of the terrible drought and dust storms, he was going to enlist in the military. I didn't want him to, and when I got back to the trailer, I took off my wedding ring and threw it. I'm afraid at seventeen, I was pretty naive and had quite a temper."

"That would fit, then," Lynne said. "Well, I'm sure you can see why we don't want to sell it."

"I understand that, but I already know what it can do. I would still like to buy it. And my plan would be to leave it to the museum when I die."

"I need to talk this over with my husband. We are both very concerned about the effects it could have. Can I call you back in a couple of days and tell you what we've decided?"

"That would be fine."

CHAPTER TWENTY-SEVEN
Lynne

AFTER OUR RETURN from our trip, we went back to our jobs, community activities, and softball games. Dinah had no ill-effects from her exposure to whatever little Betty had. The trip seemed more and more unreal.

About a week after we got home, Mother dropped by on a Saturday. "Lynne," she said, "I need your computer skills."

I raised my eyebrows. "You must be desperate. Kurt is the one with the computer skills."

"We can ask him if we need him, but I just want to do a search and see if we can find out anything about Verl James."

"Of course. Why didn't I think of that? There should be records somewhere."

I fixed us iced tea and took my laptop out to the screened porch, our favorite summertime perch. We had not made much headway when Kurt returned from the lumberyard. He suggested we may have to pay for some records. Over the next two days, we discovered that Verl James had worked on a pipeline in Alaska in the Sixties and Seventies, retired in 1990 and died from a heart attack in 1996.

Mother was the poster child for 'A Load Off My Mind'. "I can't tell you, Lynne, how convinced I was that my mother and maybe my father had something to do with his disappearance. This is such a relief."

"Oh, yes, I know. That's been very obvious over the last couple of weeks. I'm guessing they threatened him with the law or exposure, and that's why he disappeared."

"You're probably right. Of course, that doesn't answer the question of who my biological father was, but I don't think I want to know. My dad was my dad, period."

"I agree. I don't want to think of Verl as my grandfather, either. What about the attack?"

She waved her hand. "It was awful, but I put it behind me before, I can do it again. It was just such a shock, seeing him again."

Knowing my strong-willed mother, I had no doubt that she could do just that.

Dinah asked if we could do a similar search to find out what had happened to her little friend Betty.

"Do you know her last name?" Kurt asked.

"Bachmeier," Dinah said. "At least that was her mother's name."

Kurt again went in to the records and reported that he found a marriage license for Betty Bachmeier in 1965, but no record of a death certificate.

"You mean she's still alive?" Dinah said.

"It's certainly possible. You thought she was about seven or eight? That would put her in her 70s now."

"Oh, good! At least she didn't die from whatever she had."

"No, apparently, she didn't."

ANOTHER QUESTION FROM our ill-fated trip resurfaced when Dinah came downstairs one night after we thought she'd gone to bed.

She plopped on the couch, and we both looked at her with a little alarm.

"Is everything okay?" I asked.

"I just have a question. Remember when we were at that spring and made the time change?"

Kurt said, "I don't think we'll forget any time soon."

"And remember the next day when we looked at those signs about the Trail of Tears? I asked you about the picture of the guy in the turban?"

Kurt nodded.

"Well, the night before, I woke up and looked out the window. I thought I saw people in the fog. Some of the men had on turbans. Then a storm started and they disappeared. I must have been dreaming, but, before that, I didn't even know any Indians ever wore turbans."

I sat forward in my chair. "Honey, I had the same experience. I saw all those people too. Some looked like Civil War soldiers." I looked from her to Kurt. "I wonder if we didn't witness the actual time change. Maybe the ghosts of all of the people who had been in that place are there when that happens."

She said, "I thought you didn't believe in ghosts."

"I didn't. But the fact that you and I saw the same thing makes me wonder. What else would explain it?"

Kurt said, "You're both crazy."

"Fine, you tell people that we have all time-traveled, but that your wife and daughter are crazy because they've seen ghosts. See where that gets you." I gave him my sweetest smile, and he gave up. Dinah kissed us both and went to bed.

A COUPLE OF DAYS LATER, I came home to a voice message from Edna Mae Barker. She explained why she was so interested in buying our camper. I visited with her several times over the next couple of days because of something else she told me: that she had traveled back to 1939 in it.

After the shock wore off, Kurt and I spent the next couple of days discussing it. This was a scenario we hadn't considered. We had been concerned for the last two years about some unsuspecting sucker buying it and accidentally falling in to the time travel as I had. Would we consider selling it to someone who already knew what it could do? A month or two earlier, I would have answered an unqualified no, but after the Route 66 trip, I really wanted to get rid of it.

We didn't feel that destroying it was a solution because we didn't know what effect that would have on lives that had already been changed.

"But you said this woman is ninety-four? That sounds like all kinds of potential risks and problems," Kurt pointed out.

"She says she just wants to have it to sit in and remember her husband. The time travel was an accident."

"Is there a way to find out if she is—you know—of sound mind?"

"Hmmm. I wonder if the dealer there knows her. I could call him."

"I'll call him," Kurt said.

"Good idea."

WHEN HE GOT OFF the phone, he reported that Johnny Norton said Mrs. Barker was 'sharp as a tack.'

"Did he ask why you wanted to know?"

"I told him that she wanted to buy it. He wasn't surprised. Said she comes in to see it almost every day. Usually she just sits on a nearby bench, but sometimes she sits inside for a few minutes."

"Apparently he doesn't know that she slept overnight in it."

"Apparently not. I'm sure he'd be worried about the liability." He ran his fingers through his hair. "I'm not sure why we're discussing it. Seems like we should just say no."

"This woman has twanged on my heartstrings. She married her husband seventy-seven years ago. They had two children and four years later he was killed in Normandy. She has never remarried and she says that when she sits in that camper, she feels close to her husband."

"You are a softy."

"I think I have come to feel that we really can't control it. Eventually, it will end up with someone else. I think her leaving it to the museum is the best option.

"Your decision. You are the one who has told me that even the slightest change can cause trouble down the road."

"I know. I can't explain it. It just seems right."

"I have a suggestion," Kurt said, and went on to tell me.

I CALLED EDNA MAE BACK.

"If you buy our trailer, we have one recommendation —condition even."

"What is that?" Edna Mae asked.

"You told me that you have no wish to time travel in

221

it; that you just want to be able to sit in it, correct?"

"Yes, that's right." It was more like 'raht,' her voice was so soft and velvety.

"Our concern has always been that someone could time-travel accidentally and cause all kinds of changes that wouldn't be good. The best thing to do would be to install something new in the trailer. Carpet, wallpaper, a light fixture — whatever. It has to be attached to the camper. That will keep the trailer in the present."

"I can do that, or my son Dave can do it for me."

"Then we will sell it to you"

CHAPTER TWENTY-EIGHT
Edna Mae

EDNA MAE WAS THRILLED with her purchase. She allowed Johnny Norton to keep it through July and then asked him to bring it to her farm and park it behind the barn. She had already told him that she was leaving it to him in her will.

She felt a little guilty about lying to Mrs. McBriar. Now that she knew the secret about the jewelry, she could go back to 1940 when things started to get better for her and Cal. She would be able to cherish every minute of their time together.

She had a pendant that Cal had given her for their first anniversary. She had been eight months pregnant with Rosie. That August, she and Cal had taken their trailer and baby Rosie to Palo Duro Canyon. It was the best time of her life.

One day in early August, she put the pendant on and went out to the trailer after her supper. She got out the blanket and pillow and arranged them on the couch. She read for a while and then lay down on the couch and went to sleep.

THE NEXT MORNING, she again woke up with smooth skin, thick curls, and good eyesight. Once again, the camper she had bought from the McBriars was hidden behind the grove. She passed the trailer Cal had purchased sitting in the farmyard. When she walked into the house, Cal was bouncing a crying Rosie and trying to test a bottle of milk.

"Where did you go? She's been crying for twenty minutes!"

She held out her arms and took the baby, who to Cal's consternation, immediately quit crying. "I'm sorry. I woke up early and went out to do some things in the camper. Then I fell asleep again!"

He frowned. It was a little far-fetched. She wasn't one to doze off during the day, and she worried about the baby constantly.

"I'm just excited about our trip. Aren't you ready to get away?" She smiled up at him and he relented. Things had not been easy for them, and they both deserved a little fun.

They were going to pull their camper down to Palo Duro and spend a few days. Prices on the farm were getting better, but the Battle of Britain was all the newspapers could talk about. They wanted to get away from all the horror and fear.

Cal had packed the ice box with pork chops, chicken, and sausage, while Edna Mae had hauled jars of corn, green beans, okra and tomatoes to the cabinets. She also washed up a big stack of diapers for Rosie. Cal had fixed the baby a little bed in a wicker laundry basket.

Soon they were perched in the front seat of the pickup with Rosie in her mother's arms. Edna Mae couldn't help but think how shocked twenty-first century mothers would be at the lack of car seats and seat belts. But she had made this trip before in her life and knew it came out all right.

When they reached the park, they drove down the steep road into the bottom of the canyon and picked out a good site by the little stream. Cal unhooked the camper while Edna Mae sat on a stump and bounced the baby. Rosie strained her neck to look all around at the trees and walls of red rock.

"Look. She knows this place is special," she called out to Cal. He walked over, beaming at them both.

"My two beautiful girls."

Cal set up a little folding table and two chairs. Later he would start a fire and Edna Mae would fry chicken in her iron skillet. For now, they spread a blanket in the shade near the stream and played with Rosie, until she started yawning and stuffing a fist in her mouth.

Edna Mae got up and picked up the baby. "I'd better take her in for her nap."

Cal grabbed her ankle and winked at her. "Don't be long."

That was the beginning of three beautiful days. Edna Mae rigged up a wrap to carry Rosie on their hikes the way she had seen mothers in 2016 do. Cal thought she was terribly clever. They spent their days outside exploring the paths in the park, the old cabin that Charles Goodnight had built into the side of a hill when he managed a ranch in the canyon in the 1800s, and other sites. They marveled at the variety of rocks and formations. A beaver worked away in the nearby stream, and wild turkeys wandered their way around the canyon bottom. Cal pointed out a mountain lion up on the rocks. Edna Mae hoped he stayed up there.

In the evenings, after a hearty supper cooked over the fire, they watched in awe as the sunset lit up the red and gold cliffs. Then they lay on the blanket by the fire, Edna Mae cuddling Rosie and Cal cuddling Edna Mae. At night they made love on the little couch-bed with moonlight streaming through the window and Rosie snoring away peacefully in her basket on the floor beside the couch. Edna Mae clung to every moment, trying to somehow save every memory.

The last morning, Edna Mae was up early and, after checking that Rosie slumbered on, she tiptoed out of the camper and over to the stream. She perched on a rock and watched the light from the rising sun sparkling off the water.

She had a decision to make. She had planned to stay in the 1940s and relive her life. But then she realized she would have to watch Cal go off to war again and endure his loss. There would be all of the other deaths and suffering of friends and relatives. Then the struggle to raise two children on her own and the terrible tornado of 1949. She would have to be there for Rosie when her first child was still born and when Dave's first marriage ended in disaster. And on and on.

There were wonderful moments, too. But the thought of knowing ahead when and how each tragedy would occur was too much. When she saw Cal off to war the first time, there was hope that he would return safe and sound. This time she would know that would never be. She would have to sit at the baby shower given by Rosie's friends, knowing that the child Rosie carried would never wear that sleeper or play with that rattle.

Instead, she decided that every August she would come back to 1940 and take this trip again. Thinking about that would sustain her through the next year. When they returned to the farm, after Cal went to bed that night, she would sneak out to her camper hidden in the trees and return to 2016 and her older self and leave her young self at the farm.

They arrived back at the farm exhausted and sunburned. She couldn't keep her hands off Cal or tear herself away from Rosie all day. As they unpacked the camper and took care of other chores, she touched Cal so often that he began to look at her funny. In the afternoon, Cal took a sleeping Rosie out of her arms as she rocked on the porch.

However, she stuck with her resolve and returned to her own camper back in the trees after dark. She removed the anniversary pendant and her wedding ring and curled up in the bed. She felt her heart was broken

CHAPTER TWENTY-NINE

Kim

KIM HAD TRIED TO TEXT and call Edna Mae with no answer. That happened occasionally, but Kim always worried. She drove out to the farm and pulled up in front of the house.

Edna Mae's car was in the drive, and the door to the house was unlocked. Kim walked through the house calling for her grandmother. There was no answer. The coffee pot on the stove was empty and cold. Kim wondered if she should call her mother.

Then she remembered the camper. Grandma was probably out there communing with Grandpa. She smiled and shook her head. She had never known such devotion in any other marriage, even her own. She suspected that for Edna Mae, the loss of her husband at such a young age and so long ago had built him up to god-like status. That was okay. It was very sweet.

Kim let herself out the back door and walked out to the little brown and white trailer. She knocked on the door and then opened it, calling softly, "Grandma?"

Edna Mae lay curled up on the couch and didn't move. Kim bent over and touched her hand. It was cold. She had no pulse.

Kim dropped to the floor, still holding Edna Mae's hand, tears running down her cheeks. But she smiled through her tears. What a perfect end for this amazing woman.

She got up and went outside to call her mother and Uncle Dave.

ROSE ANN CALLED A DOCTOR and Dave contacted the funeral home. They arrived and supervised the removal of Edna Mae to the hearse. The doctor commented that he couldn't believe that Edna Mae could curl up that way with her arthritis.

He put his hand on Rose Ann's shoulder and said to her, Dave, and Kim, "A loss like this is never easy, but would that we could all go like Edna Mae. She kept her health to the end and has a smile on her face."

After they left, Rose Ann said to Kim, "She told me she bought this and I almost didn't believe her. Where did it come from?" She waved toward the camper.

Kim explained Edna Mae's attachment to it and how she felt close to Grandpa Cal in it. "She just wanted to come out here and sit in it. I told her she couldn't tow it."

Rose Ann climbed the steps and entered the camper. "She said they camped in one like this when I was a baby?"

Kim nodded. "She said you slept in a laundry basket."

"That's appropriate," Dave chided his sister.

Rose nodded and smiled. "It must have meant a lot to her." She turned to go out. "Huh. Look at this. I never knew her to take that ring off."

On the counter lay a gold band and an amber pendant.

THANK YOU

For taking your time to share the Time Travel Trailer's adventures. Just as the sound of a tree falling in the forest depends on hearers, a book only matters if it has readers. Please consider sharing your thoughts with other readers in a review on Amazon and/or Goodreads. Or email me at karen.musser.nortman@gmail.com.

My website provides updates on my books, my blog, and photos of our for-real camping trips. Sign up on my website for my email list and get a free download of Bats and Bones.

Go to this link:
www.karenmussernortman.com

Acknowledgments

I first must thank Dee Ann Hess, who keeps prodding me for new Time Travel Trailer books and suggested both the Route 66 and Edna Mae plot lines. Dee Ann also gave great feedback as a beta reader, along with Ginge, Marcia, Elaine, and Butch.

Trailer, Get Your Kicks is a mixture of fiction and fact. Times Beach, Steiny's, the Route 66 State Park, the Wagon Wheel Cafe, John's Modern Cabins, and the sites in Lebanon are or were real places, as are the sites mentioned on the rest of the Route 66 trip. The characters of course are fictional. Johnny Norton's museum and RV dealership is loosely based on the wonderful Jack Sisemore museum in Amarillo.

Other Books by the Author

THE TIME TRAVEL TRAILER SERIES

The Time Travel Trailer: (A Chanticleer 2015 Paranormal category winner) A 1937 vintage camper trailer half hidden in weeds catches Lynne McBriar's eye when she is visiting an elderly friend Ben. Ben eagerly sells it to her and she just as eagerly embarks on a restoration. But after each remodel, sleeping in the trailer lands Lynne and her daughter Dinah in a previous decade—exciting, yet frightening. Glimpses of their home town and ancestors fifty or sixty years earlier is exciting and also offers some clues to the mystery of Ben's lost love. But when Dinah makes a trip on her own, she separates herself from her mother by decades. It is a trip that may upset the future if Lynne and her estranged husband can't team up to bring their daughter back.

Trailer on the Fly: (An IndieBRAG Medallion Honoree) How many of us have wished at some time or other we could go back in time and change an action or a decision or just take back something that was said? But it is what it is. There is no rewind, reboot, delete key or any other trick to change the past, right? Lynne McBriar can. She buys a 1937 camper that turned out to be a time portal. When she meets a young woman who suffers from serious depression over the loss of a close friend ten years earlier, she has the power to do something about it. And there is no reason not to use that power. Right?

THE FRANNIE SHOEMAKER CAMPGROUND MYSTERIES:

Bats and Bones: (An IndieBRAG Medallion honoree) Frannie and Larry Shoemaker are retirees who enjoy weekend camping with their friends in state parks. They anticipate the usual hiking, campfires, good food, and interesting side trips among the bluffs of beautiful Bat Cave State Park until a dead body turns up. Confined in the campground and surrounded by strangers, Frannie is drawn into the investigation.

The Blue Coyote: (An IndieBRAG Medallion honoree and a 2013 Chanticleer CLUE finalist) Frannie and Larry Shoemaker love taking their grandchildren, Sabet and Joe, camping with them. But at Bluffs State Park, Frannie finds herself worrying more than usual about their safety, and when another young girl disappears from the campground in broad daylight, her fears increase. Accusations against Larry and her add to the cloud over their heads.

Peete and Repeat: (An IndieBRAG Medallion honoree, 2013 Chanticleer CLUE finalist, and 2014 Chanticleer Mystery and Mayhem finalist) A biking and camping trip to southeastern Minnesota turns into double trouble for

Frannie Shoemaker and her friends as she deals with a canoeing mishap and a couple of bodies.

The Lady of the Lake: (An IndieBRAG Medallion honoree, 2014 Chanticleer CLUE finalist) A trip down memory lane is fine if you don't stumble on a body. Frannie Shoemaker and her friends camp at Old Dam Trail State Park near one of Donna Nowak's childhood homes and take in the county fair. But the present intrudes when a body surfaces. Donna becomes the focus of the investigation and Frannie wonders if the police shouldn't be looking closer at the victim's many enemies.

To Cache a Killer: Geocaching isn't supposed to be about finding dead bodies. But when retiree, Frannie Shoemaker go camping, standard definitions don't apply. A weekend in a beautiful state park in Iowa buzzes with fund-raising events, a search for Ninja turtles, a bevy of suspects, and lots of great food. But are the campers in the wrong place at the wrong time once too often?

A Campy Christmas: A Holiday novella. The Shoemakers and Ferraros plan to spend Christmas in Texas and then take a camping trip through the Southwest. But those plans are stopped cold when they hit a rogue ice storm in Missouri and they end up snowbound in a campground. And that's just the beginning. Includes recipes and winter camping tips.

The Space Invader: A cozy/thriller mystery! The starry skies over New Mexico, the "Land of Enchantment," may hold secrets of their own. The Shoemakers and the Ferraros, on an extended camping trip, find themselves picking up a souvenir they don't want and taking side trips they didn't plan on.

We are NOT Buying a Camper! A prequel to the Frannie Shoemaker Campground Mysteries. Frannie and Larry Shoemaker have busy jobs, two teenagers, and plenty of other demands on their time and sanity. Larry's sister and brother-in-law pester them to try camping for relaxation--time to sit back, enjoy nature, and catch up on naps. After all, what could go wrong? Join Frannie as "RV there yet?" becomes "RV crazy?" and she learns that going back to nature doesn't necessarily mean a simpler life.

Happy Camper Tips and Recipes: All of the tips and recipes from the first four Frannie Shoemaker books in one convenient paperback or Kindle version that you can keep in your camping supplies!

About the Author

Karen Musser Nortman is the author of the Frannie Shoemaker Campground cozy mystery series, including several IndieBRAG Medallion honorees. After previous incarnations as a secondary social studies teacher (22 years) and a test developer (18 years), she returned to her childhood dream of writing a novel.

Karen and her husband Butch originally tent camped when their children were young and switched to a travel trailer when sleeping on the ground lost its romantic adventure. They take frequent weekend jaunts with friends to parks in Iowa and surrounding states, plus occasional longer trips. Entertainment on these trips has ranged from geocaching and hiking/biking to barbecue contests, balloon fests, and buck skinners' rendezvous. Out of these trips came the Frannie Shoemaker Campground Mysteries and now *The Time Travel Trailer* series.

More information is available on her website at www.karenmussernortman.com.

Made in the USA
Las Vegas, NV
01 February 2023

66557533R00146